The Perfect Widow

The Perfect Widow

Behind every great man is a woman

Behind his death... Even better

Deepak Trivedi

NU VOICE
PRESS

First published by NU VOICE PRESS 2025
An imprint of Hubhawks Pvt. Ltd
www.nuvoicepress.com

ISBN: 978-81-992047-2-0

Printed at Thomson Press(India) Ltd.

Published by: Nu Voice Press

For every woman who has ever been turned into a punchline, and for every silence mistaken for weakness.

This story is yours—sharp, unflinching, and unapologetic.

Table of Contents

Prologue

They say women kill with poison, that we kill with emotion. They say we crack. Snap. Bleed red over tiled floors like spilt reputation.

But that's projection. They were wrong. We don't snap. We calculate. We catalogue. That grief may look reckless, rage may look dangerous, heartbreak may look hysterical—but underneath it all, we never lose control. We gain precision. We don't lash out. We wait. We observe. We learn.

And when the time comes, and it always comes, we don't make a scene. We make a statement. We rewrite the ending with clean hands and clearer intentions than any courtroom ever documented.

We don't kill with rage. We kill with rhythm. Not in bloody footprints or bruised necklines. No. We kill in patterns. Not the kind that show up in crime scene photographs, but the quieter kind, the kind only women remember. We kill with repetition. With restraint. With every insult we don't correct, every joke we laugh at to keep the peace, every dinner party smile that tastes like rust. And if one day, our hands happen to pull a trigger or pour a drink too full, you can be damn sure that we've studied the variables, calculated the fallout, rehearsed the aftermath. By then, the eulogy will already be written.

This isn't a confession. This isn't a story about a woman driven to madness. This is a verdict delivered in lowercase, dipped in jasmine, structured like a legal brief. Clean. Measured. Undeniable. It's about a woman driven to clarity.

You think murder begins with motive. It doesn't. It begins with a moment of forgetting.

One day, I forgot to flinch when he mocked me. Next, I forgot to defend myself. Then I stopped replying. Then I stopped caring.

I remember the dinner table where his joke landed heavier than the cutlery, and I laughed anyway. I remember the courtroom whispers, colleagues quoting his satire back to me, and I swallowed the humiliation whole.

And somewhere between silence and surrender, without tantrums or ultimatums, I stopped returning to the woman I used to be. By the time I remembered, I wasn't a wife anymore. I was a file. A case. A quiet, breathing piece of evidence.

And no, you won't find blood here. No bruises. No CCTV capturing a woman lunging with a knife, shrieking something operatic.

You'll only find the faint smell of jasmine lingering in the air.

Do you know why I chose jasmine? Because grief should arrive politely. Because I knew you'd all be watching. Because murder, when done properly, should never look cheap.

They call these crimes *"intimate homicides"*. They don't just kill the man. They kill the version of the woman the world thinks she's supposed to be.

*

They used to call me *"the woman behind the man who made India laugh."*

You know him. Raghav Kapoor. Blogger turned icon. Chronicler of marital miseries rebranded as humour. Every story about me got applause. Every insult was packaged in punchlines, clapped into virality.

I was the metaphor. The meme. The moodboard of every man who wanted to mock their wife without sounding cruel.

He didn't hit me. He quoted me. Out of context. Into virality. His cruelty wore good lighting. My humiliation wore clever punchlines.

And I? I wore silence. Like a noose dressed up as jewellery.

*

I didn't kill him out of anger. That would've been too male of me.

I killed him with what he never expected: Pattern. Discipline. Calculation. Every punchline? I archived. Every joke? I timestamped. Every viral post? I dissected, frame by frame, until I learned the rhythm that made him adored.

Then I reversed them.

He built an empire on my misery. I became the editor-in-chief of his exit. He thought regret would save him. It didn't. He thought love would protect him. It didn't. He thought I wanted him dead. I didn't. I just wanted to never hear another cheap joke about myself from a stranger's mouth.

He died in a bath that still smelled like jasmine, with Coltrane playing softly, and no one to interrupt the silence but me.

And now? When they Google me, they find three things: a dead man, a bestselling book on psychological survival, and a smile no news anchor knows how to explain.

I'm not the villain here. I'm not the widow. I'm not the feminist icon they want me to be either. I'm something more inconvenient: The verdict they weren't expecting. They wanted a headline. I gave them a syllabus. They wanted catharsis. I gave them closure they couldn't swallow.

This isn't a whodunit. This is a *how-she-did-it*—invisible, elegant, inevitable.

They wanted to know what kind of woman could erase a man without raising her voice. I'll tell you. A lawyer, a widow, a ghostwriter of grief and a footnote with fingerprints. I didn't want freedom. I wanted correction. I didn't want closure. I wanted finality.

I didn't kill him with poison. I killed him with credibility. And the thing about credibility is: It doesn't need to confess. It just needs to look inevitable.

Do you know what the autopsy said? "Probable overdose. Circumstances unclear." No detective recognised my fingerprints in the silence. The world still debates whether it was an accident, a miscalculation, or a natural consequence of a life lived too loudly.

I prefer that. I prefer things to be unclear. Because clarity is for men with microphones. So, let's not pretend this is a confession. It's a verdict they'll never publish because it doesn't fit the script.

*

You want catharsis. You want a motive. You want the neat bow-tied narrative where you say, *"I get it now."* But I'm not here to be understood. I'm here to be remembered. And you? You'll try to figure out what I did. You'll speculate. You'll theorise. You'll call it cunning, cruel, calculated. You won't be entirely wrong.

But before you reach the final page, you'll realise the important question was never what I did. It was what I became while you were too busy laughing at his stories. And by then? It'll be too late. I'll already be gone—neatly filed between your suspicion, your sympathy, and your search history.

So go on. Turn the page. Underline what makes you uncomfortable. Bookmark the line where you almost agree with me. Screenshot the part where you realise you've known a man like him.

Because this isn't a murder story. It's a curriculum. And I've always been the better teacher.

And remember: Men write crime to be feared. Women write crime to be believed.

PART

One

THE PRELUDE TO A MURDER

CHAPTER 1:
The Night He Died

"He fantasised about murdering wives. I scripted a silence no one could laugh through."

Raghav Kapoor always believed midnight was sacred. A time when creativity danced with madness. He wasn't wrong. Yet tonight, midnight played executioner.

Outside our twelfth-floor apartment, Mumbai blinked and pulsed, horns distant, streetlights blurry under coastal humidity. Life moved forward. Inside, life was prepared to halt.

The playlist was soft; the lights were low. He always said jazz was the only thing that made him feel human. I preferred silence. But tonight, I played Coltrane. Not for nostalgia, but to cover the silence of death. For camouflage.

Naima floated softly into the bones of the house, spiralling through doorframes like a memory too tired to haunt properly. That slow, aching jazz, part mourning, part manipulation. The saxophone threaded itself around doorframes, trailed across the black granite kitchen counter, floated through the living room where once, during an influencer livestream, he'd called me *"intimidatingly articulate."* That clip went viral. So did the laughter. It was his sanctuary.

It was my theatre.

Steam unfurled from the bath in ribbons, curling into the jasmine oil I'd warmed precisely twenty minutes before. Jasmine. Always jasmine. The scent of Indian femininity, the perfect perfume to wrap around guilt like silk.

Citrus would've been too sharp. Lavender was too obvious. But jasmine? It smells like obedience. It smells like grace. And no one suspects death when grace is in the air. Jasmine was his favourite, too. Because, as he blogged once in *How to Kill Your Wife*, *"Jasmine: the scent that turns mourning into mythology."* How poetic, I thought. How convenient.

Tonight, it would scent the death of his satire.

He leaned against the bathroom doorframe, shirtless, a glass of Lagavulin 16 in his hand.

Aged whisky for a man who'd aged into predictability.

When I handed him the drink, his fingers brushed mine—a light, automatic touch that once meant something. Now it meant timing. He smiled, that lazy smile men develop when they think they've disarmed you.

His fingers slackened around the whisky glass like wilted punctuation. I helped him out of his jeans like an indulgent wife playing nice after a dinner argument. Button by button, zipper by zipper, like unwrapping a man too entitled to imagine consequence.

He sipped it like a man sipping applause. "Someone's in a giving mood tonight," he drawled, that cocky grin widening like a man oblivious to his expiration date. "Maybe I've been too hard on you."

There it was—the illusion of remorse. Always two minutes late, always two miles shallow.

I smiled. That old smile. The one I wore at conferences and condolence calls. It held no affection, no mercy. Just design.

"No. You should relax," I replied, watching the way his pupils subtly shrank. "Everyone deserves gentleness before sleep."

He didn't even know the whisky was measured. Three fingers. Neat. Infused with zolpidem in the dosage of a tired pharmacist. Not to kill. Not yet. Just to slow. To blur the edge between memory and finality. Between body and breath. Enough to loosen his grip on reality.

He exhaled. Sipped. I guided him into the tub like one would guide a child into a bedtime story. The bathwater was ready. Lukewarm, balanced perfectly to avoid suspicion, not too warm; no redness for the autopsy. And not cold either. Bodies fight when they're shocked. Everything from the bath salt to the towel was curated for an afterlife that needed to look curated. The candles flickered, not for romance, but for distraction, casting just enough shadow to hide my intent.

He thought I was forgiving him. Most men confuse planning with mercy. It makes them easier to bury.

He closed his eyes. Sank deeper into the water. Jazz humming. His fingers slid away from the glass, slow, like surrender.

No… this wasn't a crime of passion, I realised. It felt deliberate—like a legal document drafted not in ink, but in scent, sound, and an unsettling silence.

He gripped the tub's edge longer than usual.

"Not feeling… great," he muttered, words fusing together.

I smiled, leaned in like the dutiful wife he'd caricatured for years, and lowered him gently into the water. His breath hitched, muscles relaxing under the weight of chemicals, the room's warmth, and the steady rhythm of liquid betrayal.

Except… he blinked. Frowned. Struggled to sit upright.

Not according to plan.

My fingers hovered near the tap, ready to add hot water if needed—to tire him out, to soothe, to subdue. He looked at me, blinking harder, trying to tether himself to something coherent.

"Relax," I whispered, brushing damp hair from his forehead. "You'll feel better soon."

His fingers loosened around the glass, wrist slipping lower, knuckles grazing porcelain. His head tilted, lashes fluttering shut. The zolpidem began its final chapter, numbing, weakening, unwriting him from the inside out.

*

Once his limbs turned docile, I moved to the study. It was dimly lit, framed photos perfectly aligned, the scent of sandalwood still clinging from his last incense reel, and his MacBook Air sat open, unlocked with the fingerprint he'd never bothered to secure.

I opened a blank draft and typed slowly:

"I'm *sorry*. I tried. But some wounds don't make noise—they just echo."

I italicised '*sorry*'. Because that's what he used to do whenever he wrote something he didn't mean but wanted to sound literary.

I left the blog tab open, half-finished. A piece he'd titled *"Murder Her With Maturity."* I adjusted the brightness of the screen, wiped the keyboard with a soft cotton cloth, not because I left prints, but because I respected detail.

Behind me, something thudded. My spine straightened.

I rushed back to find the bathroom door yawning open, steam mixing with fear. Raghav had shifted, his neck angled awkwardly, fingers twitching. No unconsciousness yet. Resistance? Or remnants of a system too stubborn to collapse?

One mistake could unravel months.

I steadied myself. Sat beside the tub. Laid my palm softly on his damp forehead. "Shh… It's just the exhaustion… you're okay. Breathe easy."

He blinked up at me, confused, glassy, fragile. His lips parted. His head tilted slightly left, like a man deep in thought. Except there were no thoughts now, only neural slowing, only silence curated like content.

He mumbled a word, perhaps a name, or maybe a half-formed apology already curling up like a dead leaf on his tongue. But it didn't matter. Both would go unanswered.

I wiped my prints from the glass, tilted the photo frame on the bathroom shelf, just slightly off, like his old obsessive habit. It had to look lived-in, not staged. I folded a towel and placed it next to the bathtub, the way he'd instructed our maid to do every morning in his "self-care routines."

His body slid into the water with the ease of trust. Brotx91 had finished what zolpidem began. No gasp, no confession. Just the gentle slump of a headline collapsing into lowercase. Pulse: gone. Pupils: dilated black doors to nowhere.

More like resignation than respiration. The clock shifted to 1:42 a.m. His breathing slowed. Finally. There were no bruises, no thrashing, no sound. Only the absence that looked rehearsed.

And it was.

The thing about staged suicides is that they don't need to be tragic. They just need to be plausible. Raghav had always looked like the kind of man who thought rules were suggestions: faded college tee stretched over his wiry frame, unkempt stubble, and a mischievous glint in eyes too tired to sparkle anymore. His prematurely balding head was his least favourite joke, and yet he told it often. "Look, Aarti," he'd say, "even my follicles are abandoning me."

In death, he looked... unfinished. Like a sentence he hadn't had the last word on.

He used to say, *"If I ever go, let it look like something the New Yorker would print."*

So, I gave him that: aesthetic morbidity.

*

For a moment, when I returned to the living room, just a flicker, I remembered a winter morning in Dehradun. There was no music, no murder plans. Just a coffee mug in my hand and a frost-kissed apology in his.

"I didn't mean to become the joke you couldn't laugh at," he'd said.

I remember how the steam from the mug fogged up my glasses, how I couldn't tell if my eyes were burning from the tea or the truth. I had almost softened then.

Almost.

Tonight, that memory pressed against my mind like a cold finger, a final test of hesitation. But hesitation is a luxury. And I was now running a courtroom in my head, not a heart.

*

I checked the door: ajar enough for the maid to stumble upon the scene naturally. No one was there. No more disruptions.

At 5:57, I stood before the mirror, rehearsing. I practised devastation—subtle, measured. Not the melodrama men laugh at in WhatsApp forwards. Refined devastation. Believable. Tearless, but haunted. Brows furrowed: concern. Chin quivering: shock. Mouth parted, not too wide, not too theatrical. I tilted my head, practised the gasp, the stumble, the desperate whisper that would pull sympathy rather than suspicion. No mascara. No perfume. Just enough rawness to invoke tragedy.

At 6:02 a.m., I screamed.

Not too loud. Loud women lose credibility. Mine was *measured panic.* Shrill enough to summon neighbours. Enough tremor to suggest shock. Not hysteria. Hysterical women don't get empathy. They get sedatives and side-eyes from police reports. I almost paused, half-expecting someone to hand me a golden Oscar for Best Performance in Controlled Hysteria.

At 6:03, a faint metallic knock echoed from the service door.

Right on schedule.

I sprinted down the hallway, unbolting the door just as the maid's sandals scuffed against marble. My voice cracked on cue.

"Please—he's... he's not waking up—something's wrong—"

She gasped, dropped her keys and rushed toward him. Her bangles clinked like warning bells. *Perfect.*

She pushed past me, screaming louder than I could have managed. For a fleeting second, I was almost jealous of her performance—grief came to her naturally, while mine had to be rehearsed. The scene played itself out.

I collapsed onto the bathroom floor like it was choreographed. One hand on the tile, silk robe loose at the neck, mascara smudged, but waterproof, emotional enough, but curated.

I wept in three perfect stages: one, shock, with wide eyes, mouth parted in disbelief; two, the collapse, my knees buckling, one hand on the wall, mascara smudged just enough; and three, the whisper—raw, broken: *"He's gone."*

By 6:09, the neighbours arrived like moths, curious, whispering, calculating. Morning walkers, retired doctors, a housewife from B-703 who once DM'd Raghav for career advice. Now they whispered in slippers.

By 6:30, I wore a blanket like a war widow in silk.

By 6:45, I was an algorithm of grief.

The police arrived by 7:17. Powai police, polite but mechanical. A sub-inspector whose eyes scanned the room faster than his notes. The sub-inspector was already tired of this shift before I even said my first lie. Men in tubs don't raise red flags. They raise insurance claims. He asked the right questions, and I gave rehearsed answers.

"Did he seem depressed?"

I blinked. Once, slowly. "He hadn't been sleeping… his drinking… the pressure… the comments…" I let my voice trail off. Officers fill in the blanks when you leave enough silence.

"Was he on any medication?"

"I think he was self-medicating. Whisky helped him numb things."

"Any recent fights?"

Pause. Inhale. Blink again. "No. Actually… we'd just… reconciled."

That word hung in the air like unpaid rent. "Reconciled."

And that was it. Reconciled marriages make excellent obituaries.

"Any history of mental illness?"

"He blogged about suicidal ideation once," I said. "He said… he just joked better than he healed." That line made it into the report. His jokes about mental health became my script.

I answered everything flawlessly, with pauses in the right places, tone just enough to be tragic, never hysterical. They weren't investigating murder. They were documenting tragedy.

*

By 7:49, the paramedics carried him out.

Wrapped. Labelled. Logged. They didn't know they were filing away a man who thought cruelty was currency and satire was a shield. A man the country once adored, reduced to a silent slab of forensics.

One final applause, silent and sterile. The jasmine still lingered, now mixed with Dettol.

Death doesn't clean everything.

I sat on the edge of the bed, barefoot, silk robe still draped like an inside joke no one would ever get now, the same bed he once called *"the throne of clever domestic warfare."*

In my mind, I recited the list of things I hadn't done: no fingerprints, no poison trace outside the body, no broken glass, no bruises. Now, it was just another scene of absence. Just a man, alone in his bathtub with a half-finished blog and a full dose of irony. Some people drown in emotions; he drowned in data. Every second calibrated, every expression crafted, every reaction rehearsed.

Yet one lingering thought coiled in my mind: they'd check the whisky, but they wouldn't check the timeline. They'd ask when he drank, but they wouldn't ask who rehearsed the aftermath. Let them think grief arrived naturally, let them debate what cracked inside him. They wouldn't realise that he didn't crack. He was carefully, quietly dismantled.

And me?

I didn't swim away. I built the boat.

*

He once wrote: *"The best jokes turn tragedy into applause."*

Tonight, I wrote the last one. And nobody was laughing.

***

CHAPTER 2:
The Return from Exile

"Some women leave to escape. I returned to finish what was unfinished."

The house still remembered me. That was the problem. Not with sentiment, but with structure.

The brass doorknob had a thumb-shaped dent from where my entitlement had rested for years. Even the doormat, with its too-cheerful *Hello, Beautiful!*, curled slightly at the edges, like a smile held too long.

I stood outside the door, not knocking, not fumbling for keys, just... breathing. Breath was the only thing I could control in that moment, and I rationed it like a currency I might soon run out of.

Four months ago, I hadn't left this house like women are supposed to leave. No suitcase. No mascara streaked down the cheeks like black rivers of courage. No cinematic slamming of doors. Just a quiet, elegant exit. Like punctuation at the end of a sentence, no one wanted to hear it aloud.

People imagine women leave during tempests. Raised voices. Flying objects. Doors kicked in, neighbours peeking through curtains like crows on telephone wires. But I left in silence. The kind of silence that grows thick like damp on old bookshelves. The kind that makes you doubt whether noise was ever a real thing or just something invented by lonely people.

They thought I left because I was weak, because I broke, because *The Art of Disappearance*, his viral blog, had turned my absence into a genre.

But I didn't leave because I couldn't take it anymore. I left to watch, to see how he filled the space I once occupied, to study the contours of the cage from outside the bars.

We hadn't run out of love. That's a myth people use to anaesthetise themselves. We had run out of kindness, and that's the kind of erosion you don't notice until you cut your foot on it, bleeding quietly into the furniture.

I went to Dehradun. A place where silence isn't suspicious. I worked at an NGO helping women file protection orders against men with soft voices and sharpened egos. One woman had been beaten with her son's schoolbag because the lunchbox for her husband was packed with too little salt. Another came in barefoot, holding her divorce papers like a certificate of sin, after being locked in the bathroom with burn marks traced like confessions down her arms—her punishment for wanting to learn English. A third—pregnant, bruised, but polite, whispered that her husband only hit her on Fridays, "so the swelling would settle before Monday's temple visit."

Every case sounded like mine, only less poetic, bloodier.

Back then, I didn't want revenge. I wanted clarity. And clarity, I learned, doesn't come in the form of therapy sessions. It comes when you watch someone from the outside long enough to know how they'll end before they begin.

I didn't return because I missed him. I didn't miss the smell of his whiskey breath curled around apologies, or the way he could weaponise a compliment better than most men could weaponise fists.

I came back because he made the fatal mistake of writing to me. *"You're the only thing I ever got wrong."* He sent it like an olive branch, not realising I was the wrong tree for that olive branch.

That sentence? It earned him a second chance. At dying.

*

He opened the door wearing that grin men wear when they've read too many articles about self-improvement but skipped the parts on accountability. His beard was new. Trimmed too carefully, as if it could trim his history along with it. A paperback copy of *Daring Greatly* by Brené Brown dangled from his fingertips like a prop on a stage set slightly too small for the performance he wanted to give.

"I've changed," he said before my foot crossed the welcome mat. "I've stopped writing."

That was true, at least. His last blog post read like a confession wearing borrowed poetry, a soft eulogy to the version of himself he wanted the internet to mourn. No more jokes at my expense, no more subtweets dressed as gender critique. I was no longer *the villain with vowels*. Now I was *his mirror*.

But I didn't believe in mirrors anymore. Mirrors don't reflect the truth. They reflect light.

I believed in windows now. Windows you watch people through from a distance, windows that let you see but not touch, observe but not participate. Windows were safe. Mirrors were traps.

I walked past him, inspecting the space like a detective assessing tampered evidence. The curtains were new, but the shadows behind them weren't. The living room had been rearranged, but the corners where bitterness lingered hadn't shifted. He'd replaced the lampshade, but not the bulb that flickered above the dining table, like every promise he'd made.

I set my bag down, but didn't sit.

Memory pressed against my temples. The last night before I left hadn't been volcanic—it was surgical.

I stood by this very counter while he scrolled through his notifications, reciting likes and shares like scripture. When I finally asked for one evening without sarcasm, he didn't shout. He didn't curse. He just crafted a punchline, polished it in front of me, then tweeted it like a casual assassination.

That night, the argument didn't escalate. It deflated. I walked to the balcony, barefoot, and realised the view hadn't changed in years. Neither had he. I slept with my back turned and left the next morning while he was still dreaming of applause.

Back in the present, he moved into performance.

He made me tea. Not *chai*, but green tea. Organic. Loose-leaf. Infused with guilt and oat milk. He casually mentioned therapy the way some people mention Pilates; enough to prove a point, but not enough to show any real strain. Guilt, I've learned, is just cowardice in formalwear. It only looks like growth because it stands up straight and uses the right buzzwords.

I nodded. I smiled. I sipped the guilt. But inside, I was mapping him like a detective at a cold case wall, string and thumbtacks in my head, connecting every tremor of his fingers to the archives of the cruelty he had once called humour.

He told me about podcasts on emotional intelligence, mentioned breathing exercises, and complimented my earrings. He paused before every answer like he was proofreading his own sentences for feminist grammar mistakes. He thought we were healing. I let him think that. Healing makes men feel heroic, even when they're the ones who did the stabbing in the first place.

I stood in the mirror, studying myself. A tall frame in a beige *kurta* that had once fit better. My hair was pinned tightly into a bun, as always—neat, no strays, no stories. My eyes, though. The kohl couldn't hide the sleeplessness. The lawyer in me had always spoken in clauses; now I lived in them. Conditional. Subtextual. Watchful.

The neighbours hadn't seen me come in. Good. I wasn't ready for pity-shaped casseroles.

The silence was louder now. It echoed off the walls like an accusation. I walked into the bedroom and touched the edge of the bed where he had once sprawled like a man who owned the world. And me.

At night, we occupied separate rooms. I lay awake in the guest room, surrounded by the shadows of previous tenants, listening to his steps pacing in the hallways like a man unsure if the ghost had returned to forgive or to haunt.

On Tuesdays, he made *sabudana khichdi* like a man trying to prove domesticity could forgive character. I complimented the texture like someone offering polite applause at a recital they didn't want to attend. Dinner was podcasts and TED Talk summaries. Parsley replaced confrontation. He even brought up rescuing a dog once, as if pet ownership could serve as penance.

We did not discuss the blogs. We did not discuss what I stopped saying because of them.

We did not discuss the miscarriage or the laughter that followed it on his feed like maggots trailing a wound.

He watched me like someone tending a fire they weren't sure was safe anymore, unsure if he was supposed to warm himself or prepare for burns.

"You're different now," he said one evening, not meeting my eyes.

I looked at him slowly, gently, like one might inspect an insect they're deciding whether to kill or return to the garden.

"No," I said. "I'm just quieter."

He laughed. Softly. He shouldn't have.

On the fourth night, while he slept, I moved with the confidence of someone reclaiming stolen territory.

Behind the lower shelf of the linen cupboard, beneath forgotten winter blankets, I tucked a slim black notebook, wrapped in plain brown paper. Inside were passwords, timelines, financial records, and a blueprint: an escape, a fallback, a safeguard.

Not because I planned to leave again. But because this time, I wanted the ending to be mine.

I slid the shelf back, ensuring no trace of disruption, and stood for a moment, fingers pressed against the closed cabinet, pulse steady.

This wasn't reconciliation. This was surveillance disguised as cohabitation.

*

I told him we'd do therapy. He agreed quickly. Too quickly.

Therapy was his next act. I insisted, but he chose the venue. The therapist wore muted tones, soft scarves that looked like watercolour paintings left out in the rain. She spoke in warm vowels and practised pauses, like someone learning to knit emotions instead of just understanding them.

"Let's talk about safety," she said during our first session. "What does safety look like to you in a relationship?"

Raghav's smile could have run for political office. "We've had our issues," he said gently, "but I've been working on my emotional vocabulary."

He looked at me then, the same way magicians look at audiences right before the trick works. "I even stopped writing," he added, like that deserved applause or absolution. "Aarti's been incredible. Strong. Resilient. Maybe… too strong sometimes."

My spine straightened like someone preparing for a cross-examination.

"She doesn't yell," he continued. "She withdraws. It's like dating a constitution sometimes. So many clauses, but you never know which one you've violated."

The therapist chuckled. "That's very insightful, Raghav." She turned to me. "Aarti? Do you feel that's true?"

I inhaled slowly. Deliberately. I weighed the oxygen before spending it. "I feel like I live in a marriage where everything I say becomes a headline," I said softly. "Where my silence is mocked, and my voice is monetised."

The therapist smiled gently. Therapist Head Tilt #4: mild concern, light curiosity, smudge of patronisation. "That's very articulate," she said. "But can I ask… do you ever speak from emotion, not intellect? I think you intellectualise your pain, Aarti. It's impressive, but healing needs some messiness too. Maybe… let Raghav lead in emotional vulnerability for once?"

Raghav exhaled like a saint declining sainthood, humble and glowing. I nodded. Because arguing in rooms where women's precision is diagnosed as avoidance is a fool's game. Men cry in therapy and get called brave. Women articulate in therapy and get called repressed.

I nodded because I knew better than to wrestle with pillows and scarves.

*

On the drive home, he didn't gloat. He didn't need to.

"Even someone trained thinks you intellectualise too much," he said.

I didn't respond. I watched Powai pass by the window, with its glass buildings, latte-wielding guilt, tech bros with opinions about healing.

That night, I stood in front of the mirror. Face bare. Eyes blank. And then, just for a moment, I slipped. My throat tightened. Tears welled up, uninvited, pooling along the edges like an audience I hadn't summoned. My chin trembled, that small, dangerous betrayal of someone still hoping for a different ending.

But then I blinked. Once, slowly, and then gathered myself like closing a file.

And I whispered it. Practised it. The sentence I would eventually say aloud: "He's not breathing…"

I tried four versions: one with shock, one with detachment, once with a crack in the middle like a porcelain dish dropped from waist height and once like a prayer to no god in particular. Then I let one tear fall. Only one. Precision, not performance. Because therapy had taught him to rehearse apologies. But it taught me how to rehearse grief.

And in this house? The woman who rehearses grief always wins.

***

CHAPTER 3:
The Marriage That Silenced Her

"He never raised his voice. He raised his followers. I was bruised by applause."

The first time he humiliated me in public, it almost felt like flirting. Almost charming, in that brittle way, cruelty sometimes wears charisma like an old borrowed suit.

It was a dinner party in Bandra—one of those Mumbai nights where everyone smells slightly of ambition, subtle perfume, and unpaid EMIs. The wine was cheap, the conversation expensive. The room sparkled with media freelancers who wrote columns they hadn't read, junior lawyers pretending to hate networking, and a television actress who positioned herself perfectly under the warm glow of a designer floor lamp while pretending she didn't care about being noticed.

I brought a bottle of Merlot. He brought a punchline.

"Aarti's taste in poetry is so intense, even Sylvia Plath would say: *Girl, relax.*"

The room laughed the way middle-class liberals always laugh when they smell cleverness, even if they can't find the map to it. A wave of performative laughter swept across the polished floors, bouncing off hanging plants and ethically sourced furniture.

I smiled too-the kind of smile women wear when they've learned early that not all knives shine. The kind that says: *Don't flinch now. Not yet.*

Under the table, his hand squeezed my thigh. Firm. Possessive. Not lust. Ownership. Punctuation. That was his favourite style of cruelty: the cruelty that got likes. The cruelty that sounded like culture.

That was the thing about Raghav: his cruelty didn't arrive in shouts or slaps. It came gift-wrapped in hashtags, applauded by strangers who thought they understood 'funny feminist husbands'.

A few days later, at Café Artisan, while I stirred overpriced chamomile tea, a colleague from chambers tapped my shoulder.

"Hey… you're Raghav Kapoor's wife, right?"

I nodded cautiously.

She chuckled, showing me her phone. "That viral post… absolutely savage."

It was his latest: *"Marriage tip: if your wife out-earns you, just make her orgasm during tax season. That way, at least someone's getting returns."*

Her screen showed 19,000 likes. The retweet count blinked like a courtroom timer ticking down my credibility.

My jaw tightened. "I haven't read it."

Her smile faltered. "Oh… well… it's obviously just jokes… You're a good sport about it, right?"

I paid the bill without tasting my tea. Outside, I deleted the last backup folder titled 'His Side of the Story'.

That was just the trailer. The feature film came later, online.

He wrote about me the way city columnists write about bad weather: with polished irritation, dressed in metaphor, careful not to mention names, careful to leave breadcrumbs.

My favourite was the one about the pitch meeting I missed because I was bleeding through my jeans and hiding it with layers of black fabric.

"Hormonal weather conditions," he wrote. "Like, you know, how sudden rain cancels cricket? Except in this case, it cancels PowerPoint decks." Seventeen thousand likes. Bookmarked in boardrooms where men wore fitted shirts and opinions about reproductive rights.

Another piece followed: "She only orgasms when she out-bills me."

That one made it to a podcast. My managing partner quoted it at my next review, half-smiling. "No names. But hilarious, right?"

No, Raghav never said I was incompetent. That would have required direct confrontation, and men like him didn't bruise women with fists. They bruised women with context. With applause.

The world forgives beautiful abusers. Especially the ones who remember to end their sentences with soft chuckles and links to their Patreon.

The next morning, he published: "Chop Her Ego". No names, of course. He was too clever for that. But everyone knew. That's the point. *"She enters courtrooms like they're coliseums. I've seen her cross-examine my libido like it's hostile witness testimony."* 23,000 likes. Sent to me by colleagues who thought it was "cheeky."

One said: "He's brilliant, Aarti. Tell him to write a novel."

He already had. I was the manuscript.

*

I tried to speak once. Not loudly. Not in front of friends. Quietly. Behind closed doors. Just him, me, and a ceiling fan making tired revolutions overhead, like an old guard pacing a shift no one wanted.

He tilted his head the way men tilt when they want to look curious but stay above correction. "It's satire, babe. People love couples who can laugh at each other."

What he meant was: *They love me. They love me for mocking you. You should thank me for making you interesting.*

The worst part wasn't what he said. It was how beautifully he said it. Perfect pacing. Clean punchlines. A rhythm built not from rage but from craftsmanship.

The world doesn't forgive men for being violent. It forgives them for being clever. And clever cruelty is the kind no one wants to cancel, because it looks too much like art when it's filtered correctly on Instagram.

*

Loss came next. But not the cinematic kind. No dramatic scenes. No shattered mugs or bloodstains you can scrub with Domex.

It was a Wednesday. Cloudy but not important. Just humid enough for your jeans to stick to your knees when you sit for too long. The kind of day that slips between calendars and never gets remembered.

I'd been bleeding for two days. Google said, *"Implantation bleeding."* Then *"Possible miscarriage."* Then: *"Prepare yourself."* Clinical, quiet, indifferent.

By the time the cramps hit hard enough to drop me to the bathroom floor, the ceiling fan was still turning. Still keeping time like a god who's bored of intervening. Just warm blood and cold marble.

I curled up on the bathroom floor. Bit into a towel so the grief wouldn't echo.

There was no ultrasound photo. No heartbeat to mourn. Just… something gone.

Outside, I could hear him practising a podcast. His voice crisp, clear, media-trained: "Men are expected to be fathers before they're even ready to be boyfriends. Isn't that wild?" He laughed at his own cleverness. The same way he paused for laughter, even in empty rooms.

He passed the door twice. "Babe," he called through the thin air, "if you're using the water heater, save some pressure. I've got a Zoom at 4."

It wasn't the pain that made me bite harder. It was the knowledge that he had heard something. And chosen to ignore it.

I bled. He posted.

Later, he'd write: *"Satire is just grief wearing a funny hat."*

Top comment? "Your wife sounds terrifying. Marry me next."

No one saw the timeline. The body unmaking life while he crafted engagement. I didn't tell him. Not because I was afraid. But because some grief doesn't deserve an audience.

*

He didn't believe women belonged in the kitchen. He believed in quoting them until they disappeared.

My boundaries became punchlines. My silence? "Tense feminine energy." My grief? "Performance anxiety."

"She's a feminist Gita with Wi-Fi," he wrote once. "Our foreplay now includes a Google Calendar sync."

He turned me into shareable shame. The world adored him for it. The way they adore clever cruelty when it's dressed in lowercase fonts and sarcasm.

The world doesn't cancel charming men. They follow them.

*

Later, I changed the sheets myself, scrubbed the towel, and rinsed the bathroom floor with disinfectant. But the blood stayed, a faint watermark only I could see.

At dinner, he handed me the salt. "You look exhausted. Long day at court?"

I nodded. "You could say that."

We ate in silence. I didn't tell him about the test, the towel, or the bleeding. I didn't explain why I stopped drinking the herbal tea that came with packaging marked *safe for pregnancy*.

One week later, another blog: "Bury Her Nagging Habit": Twenty-one thousand likes. Four thousand shares. He never asked about the blood, never noticed the discarded pills, never questioned why the scent of soap changed in the bathroom.

I didn't offer explanations. Because if a man needs a punchline, he doesn't deserve the whole story.

In my journal, I wrote: *"Some women lose children. I lost the part of me that believed in nurturing anything again. My body gave up. My voice followed. And that… was the beginning of my internal divorce."*

*

It wasn't one wound. It was a dozen paper cuts, daily. Accidental on the surface, intentional underneath. It was a quiet disconnection, like someone unplugging a machine gently before walking away. The last time I cried in front of him, I was naked and invisible, water scalding, soap in my mouth. My voice was caught somewhere between a scream and an apology.

He knocked, didn't hear me. He heard something and chose to ignore it. It wasn't cruelty. It was scheduling.

Something in me didn't break. It disconnected, like someone turning off the mains in a house full of working lightbulbs. I didn't say goodbye. I said nothing. I wasn't his wife anymore.

I was set dressing. Background noise. A woman-shaped mood board for his cleverness. The "strong, high-strung lawyer wife" who couldn't take a joke. That's how he cast me in his one-man play.

So, I stopped arguing. I started rehearsing grief like other women rehearse lullabies. Three nods at parties, one laugh per joke, mascara only on the top lashes: clean, corporate, almost human.

I became his background music. A smart woman-shaped prop in his monologue.

He thought he was the comedian. He didn't know he was already reading lines from a script I had authored. One where the applause would stop halfway through the performance. And the lights? They would go out mid-sentence.

He thought I was mourning. I was mapping. He thought I was leaving emotionally, and I had. But not without backing up the entire hard drive first.

***

CHAPTER 4:
The Trigger Post

"He wrote to trend. I wrote to terminate."

It dropped just after midnight. Always midnight. That was his favourite trick: cruelty arrives better when dressed like poetry, timed with insomnia, disguised as insight. Men like Raghav don't post during the day, when things are busy, when people have bills to pay, commutes to suffer, deadlines looming like unpaid debts. They post at midnight, when shame wears a different shape, and algorithms serve heartbreak like a curated playlist.

This one was worse than the others. Not cleverer. Just sharper, like he'd finally filed the teeth of his cruelty into something elegant. His blog. *Duct Tape and Divorce Papers.* No all-caps. No shock value. Just lowercase venom and curated cruelty in font sizes soft enough to be mistaken for tenderness.

Clever. Clickable. Cruel. He no longer wrote about politics. No more movie reviews. No trending takes on world issues. Just one subject. Me. He'd made a career out of misnaming me so perfectly that even strangers could spell my humiliation without ever hearing my voice. Paragraph after paragraph of carefully engineered injury.

"She once ghosted me in the same house. Not a suitcase touched. Just a haunting in human form", "She doesn't yell. She amortises your self-esteem across fiscal quarters."

It wasn't satire. It was psychological necrophilia: dragging a woman's reputation through clever metaphors so often, she becomes a literary corpse everyone wants to quote.

*

I should have slept. But the blog glowed on my screen like a confession set to ambient lighting. I scrolled past the 9,000 likes and the sea of comments from men who wore feminism like cologne: just enough to smell nice, not enough to choke on.

And then the line that started catching fire before I even finished reading it: *"Ever argued with a high-functioning, low-empathy corporate lawyer at 2 a.m.? Don't. She doesn't yell; she destroys your income bracket."*

By the time I reached the bottom of the post, that single sentence alone had been reposted over seven thousand times. Instagram screenshots. WhatsApp forwards. Twitter threads written by media interns who drink oat milk and claim to love dark women but only follow influencers with mirror selfies and NGO hashtags.

I sat in bed in the blue glow of the screen, that particular kind of glow that makes you look like a statue in someone else's museum. My legs were cold under the blanket. I didn't adjust it. I let the cold sit with me like a witness no one else could see.

And then came the closing line. The one that would be quoted the most, looped endlessly in reels and reaction videos and late-night tweet threads written by men who call themselves feminists but still interrupt their girlfriends in bookshops.

"She didn't kill the marriage. She euthanised it. Painless. Precise. Like a woman filing income tax returns, without exemptions."

I laughed. Not from humour, but from clarity. This wasn't defamation. This was craft. He'd finally found a way to make my collapse go viral.

Mumbai is small. The professional world is even smaller. WhatsApp groups were basically villages with Wi-Fi. Everyone already knew. Colleagues, friends, clients. They didn't need my name; they needed the story. And he'd handed them one, like a child handing a loaded gun to the wrong friend.

He used to say I was too poised to bleed. So, he decided to bleed me out in paragraphs instead. One hyperlink at a time.

"If I die," he wrote, "she won't cry. She'll reorganise the funeral itinerary for efficiency."

Twelve thousand shares. Top comments: "Oof. She sounds terrifying. But hot," "He's basically married to a court notice."

What none of them knew, what even *he* didn't know, was that I'd already written his funeral itinerary. Venue. Caterer. Guest list. RSVP spreadsheet. I'd written two drafts of the eulogy: one polite, one brutal. It wasn't revenge. It was a rehearsal.

*

Three weeks later, the consequence hit home.

Mid-trial prep, my boss called me in, his voice clipped, tone guarded. "There's been… feedback," he began, shifting in his chair. "Your spouse's content is… visible. To clients."

He didn't have to elaborate. The clip from Raghav's podcast was circulating on LinkedIn: *"Marriage to a lawyer teaches you cross-examination… in bed too."* A client had forwarded it with a line: *"Conflict of interest much?"*

I kept my spine straight. "My work stands on merit."

He gave me the corporate smile of men who pretend gender bias is a myth. "Of course. But perception… perception can be tricky."

I'd been sidelined from a career-defining case.

The next morning, I stepped into court like a woman walking on invisible ashes.

At chambers, my junior Riya dropped a folder on my desk with a grimace. "I'd be careful if I were you. The Delhi Arbitration Conference just dropped your keynote."

My inbox confirmed it:

Subject: Reputation Risk Reassessment.

Body: "Given circulating media narratives, we are reviewing speaker suitability."

Translation: Your dignity is now a trending liability.

It was official. His jokes weren't just likes; they were liabilities now.

My career was collateral in his comedy routine. Not fired, not disciplined. Just reallocated.

The beautiful HR word for *evaporated.*

My pending promotion, which had been "green-light pending" for three months, turned grey in silence. No formal rejection. No explanation. Just silence. The kind of silence you don't fight because you can't even prove where the sound used to be. Just a space where ambition used to be.

At noon, I was called into the managing partner's office.

He had the voice, men use when speaking to women they label "brilliant, but..." The slow-pour voice. The condescending calm. "Aarti… this isn't about your capability. We all respect your work. This is more… about perception."

I nodded slowly.

He continued: "High-conflict litigation requires mental endurance. Emotional resilience. The current media chatter, even though it's technically anonymous, has raised some… questions."

I smiled. Tilted my head five degrees left. The sarcasm sweet spot. "You mean: am I mentally stable enough to deal with men like me?"

He blinked and didn't laugh. I hadn't intended it as a joke.

Silence. Which is how corporate institutions say: *"We expected you to collapse prettier."*

*

That evening, I didn't go home. I sat in the car outside the office for forty-two minutes, holding the keys, engine off, watching the thin sliver of Bandra traffic crawl past like someone else's dream unfolding without permission. No music. No podcasts. Just my own breath and his voice playing in my head, over and over, like someone had set my skull to *repeat* and lost the password.

By the time I finally walked into the flat, he was on the couch, legs up, scrolling, scrolling, scrolling. Laughing softly to himself like a boy watching someone else get into trouble at school. He didn't even look up.

I confronted him that evening. Not with fury, but cold, prosecutorial precision. "I lost a case," I said simply, standing in the kitchen while he scrolled on his phone.

His brows knitted, feigning confusion. "That's awful. Did they screw up the filing?"

I dropped my phone onto the counter, screen open to his tweet.

His shoulders stiffened. "Oh… that. It's harmless. Everyone knows it's satire."

"Clients don't," I said. "Senior partners don't."

"Babe," he said, stepping closer, "this is how I built a brand. You knew who I was."

I stepped back. "No. I knew who you pretended to be. There's a difference."

He scoffed, voice defensive. "Why can't you laugh with me?"

I met his gaze, steady and unforgiving. "Because you made sure everyone laughed *at* me."

I stood in the doorway and looked at him the way morticians must look at men who died with good teeth but bad hearts.

There was a photograph on the side table. Our wedding photo. Him in a light grey *sherwani*, smiling like a man who had just beaten traffic to his own destiny. Me in red. Eyes open, not quite smiling, just tired from fabric and tradition. His hand over mine, his eyes on me. Like he knew I'd blink first.

I picked up the frame. Traced the metal edge with one thumb. Held it the way people hold something they've already decided to drop later.

"This man is killing me with satire," I whispered to myself, quiet enough that even the furniture leaned closer to hear. "I can't live with him anymore."

It didn't feel like anger. Anger is noisy. This was clarity.

I stood there with the photograph while he grinned into his screen, already rehearsing his next one-liner. The next applause. The next clever headline. He didn't even notice I was holding the frame.

It didn't need to be a fight. There wouldn't be tears. There wouldn't be smashed plates or raised voices or screaming fits that neighbours would pretend not to hear. There would just be the click of a folder opening, a plan resuming, of tabs opening like windows in a building I was already setting on fire, one floor at a time. I toggled my mind like browser tabs. Grief was to be minimised, rage was to be paused, and clarity was to be put on full screen.

This wasn't murder. Murder is what men commit when they don't know how else to win. This was something better. This was closure. Silent. Symmetrical. Precise. He thought he was trending, but I was planning his extinction.

***

CHAPTER 5:
The First Spreadsheet

"Some women cry in bathrooms. I kept data."

I had lunch the next day with Dev—Raghav's oldest friend, a supposed neutral zone in our history. Except today, his smile was tight, his eyes sharper. The café hummed with casual Mumbai chaos, clattering cutlery, office gossip, and the low thrum of playlist pop.

Dev looked like he'd stepped out of a monochrome magazine spread on postmodern grief. Ironically rumpled charcoal shirt, dark jeans without visible branding, and tortoise-shell glasses that managed to soften his otherwise calculating stare. His beard was neatly trimmed, as if curated for trustworthiness. Always two watches: an Apple Watch on one wrist, a dead Fitbit on the other. "For vibes," he always said. Time, after all, was an aesthetic.

"Looks like someone's wife is trending again," Dev said, sliding his phone across the café table, open to Raghav's latest viral thread.

I stayed composed, stirring my iced coffee. "You think it's funny?"

Dev's grin faltered. He leaned in. "Honestly? No. It's starting to get… ugly."

My eyebrow lifted. "Starting?"

He hesitated, then whispered, "Aarti, you didn't hear this from me… but brands are pulling out of his next event. HR flagged some posts after the podcast rant."

Something in my chest loosened. Not joy, but… calculation. "Good," I said simply.

Dev blinked, surprised at my flatness. He studied me a beat longer, his gaze lingering on my relaxed posture. "You've changed," he muttered, like it made him uneasy. And he was right. I wasn't the wife anymore. I was the architect.

*

That evening, back home, Raghav swanned in mid-rant.

"Cancel culture is just bored people looking for targets," he snapped, slamming his laptop shut.

I scrolled through my phone without looking up. "Targets usually scream when they're hit."

He ignored the jab, pacing like a king wounded by peasants. "Nothing I've said is personal. I don't even name you."

"That's what makes it worse," I replied, quiet and direct. "You erased me so cleanly, they forgot I had a name."

*

At midnight, I sat in the dark, staring at his latest thread. The cursor blinked in a blank message box, waiting.

I debated with myself.

This was childish. Petty. Creating a fake account just to jab at him online? It felt beneath me. A parody of resistance. But then again, wasn't that what he counted on? That I'd keep playing dignified while he strip-mined our life for content?

I'd tried directness. I'd tried silence. I'd even tried conversation over dinner, met only with smirks and another joke queued for his blog. But he didn't hear words. He heard audience reactions. And the only language he respected was virality.

So, I did what I once swore I never would.

I created a throwaway handle, a sterile avatar with no history. And under his smug blog post, I typed: *"Curious… didn't your wife win the gender bias PIL last year? Yet here you are, monetising her life story without credit."*

I logged off.

The thread imploded within hours.

Screenshots circulated, blogs dissected his 'feminist husband' brand. Old podcast clips resurfaced. By morning, he was hashtagged: #ContentAtHerCost. His phone wouldn't stop buzzing. Neither would his ego.

He looked at me over breakfast, perplexed. "What the hell… why is everyone… turning?"

I smiled serenely. "Maybe people are learning to read between punchlines."

That night, the spreadsheet evolved. No smashed glass. No dramatic slump against a doorframe, mascara streaking in elegant ruin like actresses in indie films. No primal scream that could rattle windowpanes or make neighbours shift uneasily behind curtains.

Grief is never as photogenic as people hope it might be. It's not operatic. It's just… administration.

I sat at my desk beneath the kind of white light that exposes flaws in furniture, in skin, in memory. That sharp, clinical glow that makes even hope look poorly manufactured. The room smelled faintly of turmeric from dinner, jasmine from old hair oil, and something else entirely: the slow corrosion of someone becoming someone else.

The screen was already open, the cursor blinking like a heart monitor, steady, unsentimental, unsupervised. The gentle, mechanical pulse of expectation.

I wasn't even supposed to be awake. I should have been asleep, curled on my left side like every article about fertility advises, imagining positive pregnancy tests or beachfront vacations or something more marketable to the life I used to believe I could have. Instead, I sat in that brittle light, scrolling through the comments under his previous posts.

"Her kisses taste like prenups," "She once ghosted me in the same house,""She only orgasms when she out-bills me."

Eleven thousand six hundred seventy-two likes. Hundreds of comments. Half of them were anonymous. Half of them were probably people we'd met once, at someone's cousin's engagement party, sipping overpriced whiskey in someone's balcony with the good fairy lights.

He hadn't named me anywhere. That was the genius of it. Just enough breadcrumbs to keep plausible deniability intact. Wife jokes. Clever hints. Legal references were scattered like expensive confetti. People filled in the blanks the way a bored child finishes mazes on restaurant menus.

And me? I wasn't a person anymore. I was material, content, a meme, a joke they laughed about in group chats, the "cold courtroom wife" who couldn't take a joke.

The silence after public ridicule is the loudest thing you'll ever hear. I sat with it for a while, letting that sick flavour roll around my tongue like something medicinal I'd forgotten how to swallow. Then I opened a new Excel sheet. No flourish. No title yet. Just that familiar endless grid of pale grey lines stretching into digital nothingness, perfect and empty, like freshly prepared ground before a burial. The blood hadn't even fully left me. But his sarcasm had already been packaged, captioned, and monetised.

I didn't want to confront him. Confrontation is for women still hoping to be heard. I had stopped performing for the jury.

I opened a new document. There were no tears, just rows and formulas. The cursor blinked—the only thing in that house still responding to me without irony.

*

Then, methodically, like a woman quietly drawing a battlefield with scented ink and surgical gloves, I began to type.

Not quickly. Not like a woman possessed. Slowly. Carefully. The way architects start with load-bearing walls before thinking about balconies. The way coroners gently unfold body bags before naming the cause of death. I typed like someone drawing a map of a battlefield, not with crayons, but with gloves on. With soft, deliberate precision.

Date. Humiliation. Public Reaction. His Excuse. My Response. Alternate Ending.

It wasn't revenge. It wasn't even anger. It was… archaeology. Digging up something that had been dead for years but preserved beneath layers of expensive candles, careful Instagram captions, polite smiles at brunches where no one really listens to each other anyway. A museum of micro-deaths, neatly labelled.

The first entry was easy. That dinner in Bandra. The poetry joke. The way his fingers squeezed my thigh, gentle enough to look like affection, firm enough to say *don't make this awkward.* Applause. Laughter. Instagram stories with martini emojis and hashtags about "couple goals." His excuse? "It's satire, babe. You were brilliant."

My response? Half a smile. I changed the topic to housing prices. Something neutral. Something safe.

Alternate Ending? I stand up. I tell him to leave the table. I stay. Alone. Strong. Cinematic.

But life is not cinema. Life is exit strategies filed under folders you don't label "revenge," because you don't want your hard drives seized.

Another row. Another joke. "She files her emotions under Schedule C." Eight thousand seven hundred likes. Memes. GIFs.

He told me later: "It's just character work, Aarti. You inspired the bit." As if I should've been grateful for being immortalised as the punchline of my own erasure.

By entry number seventeen, I stopped counting. Each cell filled like drops of venom measured in millilitres, one by one, slow, deliberate, clinical. This wasn't a journal. Journals are for grief you don't want anyone else to read. This was an audit. Of humiliation. Of a disappearing act performed in public, under applause.

*

He knocked on the door that night.

"Babe, you up? I forgot the WiFi password again."

I didn't answer. He'd written "Smother Her with Silence" after my dad died, and I went mute for weeks. He'd penned "Poison Her with Kindness" when I stopped laughing at his rape joke. He blogged "Chop Her Ego" the week I won a case he lost. Each metaphor was a scalpel. He had carved me up into paragraphs, so I responded in cells.

By the time the clock blinked 3:40 a.m., the file had a second tab: EXIT STRATEGY. Secure offshore savings, schedule a consultation with Kabir (lawyer, college friend); alias email: a.mehra.inbox@gmail.com, backup marriage records, medical notes, screenshots, pre-draft custody clauses and future-proof the fallout, and finally, erase non-essential digital traces.

There was no mention of vanishing. Just choreography. An escape plan dressed as peace.

*

At dawn, curiosity pushed me into his drafts folder. In his archives, hidden between drafts and deleted tags, was a blog I remembered too well. He had almost trashed it But didn't.

"If she ever disappears, maybe silence will finally feel like peace."

He thought it was poetic. I knew it was a prophecy. He thought I hadn't read it. I had. Five times. Enough to make it a footnote in my affidavit if needed.

*

I hovered over "Save As." *Plan?* No. Too cold. *Revenge?* Too theatrical. *Diary?* Too soft. *Therapy?* Please.

I typed: *Alt_Life_v2.xlsx*. Alternate life. Second draft. Not a sequel, because I wanted an ending that belonged to me, not the algorithm.

They say hurt people hurt people. It's printed on coffee mugs now, quoted in trauma blogs, and handed out like consolation prizes to women expected to collapse attractively. No. Hurt people don't hurt people. Hurt people build systems. And I was always better at systems than at screaming in stairwells, no one would remember the next day.

*

Dev called two days later.

"Listen… I don't know what you're planning, but I can smell a storm."

"Do you want to take cover, Dev?" I asked coolly.

Silence crackled on the line.

"I… I didn't think it was this deep," he admitted.

I closed my laptop with calm finality. "You should've noticed earlier."

*

At midnight, I sat by the window, watching Mumbai's restless skyline.

Raghav thought he had written the marriage script. He thought going viral was the goal. He thought followers were safety nets.

But I had something better than applause. I had evidence. And unlike applause, evidence doesn't fade when the lights go out.

***

CHAPTER 6: The Vanishing That Failed

"Some women run. Some return. I did both. And now? I don't ask permission to vanish. I just make sure they can't trace the exit."

They always get it wrong. Sometimes, women don't run. They *vanish*. Not into shadows, but into silence. Not into forests, but into plausible deniability, prayer flags, and "wellness."

I didn't vanish like a ghost. I disappeared like a verdict. Yoga retreats, reflections, #rebirth. It wasn't an escape. It was a *strategy*. Every WhatsApp reply was measured, every weekend booking a breadcrumb. Every conversation with Raghav? A mirror held just long enough to let him see *nothing*.

Because I didn't want to leave him. I wanted him to rot in the silence he curated.

But here's the thing about perfectly written endings: They attract editors.

*

You want the truth? Fine.

I didn't vanish because I was scared. I vanished because he wasn't.

Raghav had turned me into performance art. A blog muse. He posted my breakdowns like they were movie trailers. My grief had punchlines. My silences were stylised in italics. And the internet applauded.

So, one sticky August Thursday, I flipped the script. He'd written my pain. Now I'd write *his downfall.*

*

It started as a fantasy. As soft and slippery as daydreams get. But the more Raghav blogged, the more I outlined. Every jab. Every metaphor. He said marriage was "emotional claustrophobia."

Funny. Because I was suffocating too, just quietly.

So, I stopped trying to *speak*. And started planning how to *vanish.*

*

My exit was designed in layers. Each move calculated, each absence explained.

"Yoga retreat," I told him over a bland dinner while he drafted another post mocking my courtroom victories.

"Detox program," I texted old friends who'd stopped calling after his third viral podcast.

"Self-care," I posted on WhatsApp groups that had stopped inviting me after I became the courtroom caricature.

Every message was rehearsed. I wasn't slipping away; I was constructing my absence like an alibi.

Nirvan Ashram was my stage. Every visit, a rehearsal. Every silent chant, a lie with folded legs. That's where I met Varun. Slippery-eyed, socially awkward, desperate to be useful. His glasses were always smudged, his eyes watery and restless. He blinked often, like the world was too bright. Spoke in half-sentences, never quite completing thoughts. Not a lover, not even a co-conspirator. Just an over-enthusiastic disciple of Raghav's public humiliation comedy.

He called himself a "fan" of Raghav's blogs. Red flag.

He wasn't dangerous. Just… inconvenient. He was quiet, twitchy, eager—the kind of man who thinks listening is affection and stalking is devotion. I used him. He thought he was saving me, and I let him believe that. He wasn't the lead. He was the prop.

*

Disappearance wasn't impulsive: it was a legal strategy disguised as self-care.

The plan was designed in silence: Nirvan Ashram, withdrawal from digital footprints, a corpse without a name, swap the IDs, and a suicide note without death. It was supposed to be a clinical, clean exit, no messy aftermath.

I even practised the suicide note in my own handwriting: *"I couldn't live in the silence anymore. You wrote my death."* Poetic, isn't it? The kind of line Raghav would've blogged with three hashtags and a moody filter. I thought it was perfect. He'd be arrested, his satire would be used as evidence, and I would rise, elsewhere, unknown but free. Spoiler: Perfection is ego dressed in choreography.

*

I should have anticipated Dev. Raghav's best friend, a college ghost. The man who loitered around our marriage like a silent spectator. At first, Dev was logistics: falsified paperwork, cadaver, burner phones, cash drops, forged records. A professional saboteur.

"Let's make him rot," Dev had said, eyes gleaming with vengeance. "I'll handle the switch. You just disappear."

I trusted him enough to pack one bag and leave. That was my only mistake. I shouldn't have. Because Dev didn't hate Raghav's cruelty. He envied his spotlight.

*

At first, he was helpful. Then… curious. *Too* curious. His ambiguity wasn't accidental. It was engineered. He never said what he wanted—only what *we* needed. But the 'we' was always his version. His gaze lingered too long. His admiration was sticky. He began quoting Raghav's posts like scripture.

"At what point does love become a cage?" he asked one night. That line changed me. His eyes glowed; not with empathy, but with ownership.

*

I was packed. The switch was ready. We left the city in an unmarked hatchback, dusk bleeding into the highway.

Dev kept the music low. The playlist was instrumental: jazz, or something that wanted to be. Between notes, he glanced at me too often. His profile was a study in curated ease: a faint five o'clock shadow he knew looked good in photos, buttoned shirt sleeves rolled halfway up his forearms, the same twin watches on his wrists

"It's poetic, you know?" he murmured, eyes fixed on the road. "You… vanishing like smoke, while Raghav gasps for air."

I smiled, rehearsed, fingers curling around the car door handle, more memory than movement. The prickle at the base of my spine wasn't fear—it was a checklist. Had I wiped the hard drives? Logged out of every cloud? Did I hide that one court memo with my name printed too clearly? I played each loose thread like a prosecutor prepping cross-examination.

And beneath all that, a different unease.

I trusted Dev… didn't I? He had been precise. Generous. Unflinching. Was that romanticism or a warning?

By the time we reached the hills, my phone was gone, SIM discarded, my identity reduced to initials on a check-in ledger. Two days. That was the agreement. Disappear, fake the death, escape to the next phase.

*

But on the third morning, I woke up wrong.

The air was too still. My limbs were too heavy. The clock blinked 11:00 a.m., but my last memory was falling asleep at nine. No phone. No exit.

Dev stood at the window, humming to himself, unshaven and too comfortable. "Change of plans," he said smoothly. "We're staying longer. You need time… to detox."

The walls pressed in closer.

*

Dev transformed from co-conspirator to captor without raising his voice. No ropes. No chains. Just endless herbal teas laced with something numbing. Detox plans I hadn't signed up for. His stories spiralled from 'saving me' to 'saving us'.

He quoted Raghav's old blogs, twisting them, romanticising them, weaponising them.

"I don't want you to be erased," he whispered one night. "I want you… reborn. As mine."

His hand brushed mine accidentally, then stayed there a second too long.

"You're really going through with this, huh?" he said.

"Through with what?" I asked.

"The rewrite," he smiled, but something in it was off. It wasn't admiration. It was a rehearsal.

I should have seen it before. He wasn't a side character. He was testing his lighting for the lead role. He wasn't helping me escape Raghav. He was helping himself escape anonymity.

*

The retreat staff believed every word.

"She's fragile," Dev explained. "Her husband… media scandal… breakdown."

They nodded sympathetically, bringing me meals I didn't touch, booking therapy sessions I refused to attend.

No Wi-Fi. No network. No exits. Every attempt to ask for help was intercepted, smothered under a narrative I hadn't written but was forced to star in. Dev's gaze followed me everywhere, controlling without touch, possessive without violence.

I was a missing woman no one was looking for.

*

And then, the twist I didn't write.

On the ninth day, just before midnight, the door creaked open. I tensed, expecting Dev.

It was Raghav.

Pale. Hollow. Unshaven. The man who once blogged my silence now stared at it.

We stared at each other—former enemies, accidental witnesses to each other's destruction.

He whispered, *"Aarti?"* I blinked. Twice. "You're alive," he whispered, like he wasn't sure if it was relief or fear.

I couldn't speak. Because what do you say when the man who made you disappear… becomes the one to rescue you?

*

The unravelling wasn't cinematic. It was jagged, noisy, and impossible to control.

The headline came before dawn: *Satire Blogger's Friend Accused in Wife's Disappearance.* I caught snatches of my own name in taxi radios, the syllables mispronounced but sharp enough to sting.

In the court lobby, a journalist with a crooked press badge shoved a recorder at me. "Ma'am, do you feel safe now?"

In the next corridor, I passed Dev being led away by two plainclothes officers, his wrists swallowed by the glint of handcuffs. He smirked when he saw me, like the whole thing was an inside joke only he understood.

Police statements bled into affidavits. Raghav's blog posts appeared on projector screens in courtrooms; each line stripped of irony until they looked like confessions. Screenshots from WhatsApp groups became exhibits, the emojis suddenly sinister.

I stood where once they'd caricatured me, this time dictating the narrative. Every question directed at me was a thread I could pull, and I tugged until the courtroom fabric frayed.

At night, I scrolled through the chaos under a single desk lamp, bookmarking every post, every accusation, every moment where public opinion bent just slightly in my favour. It wasn't a victory yet.

*

Do I regret it?

Not the architecture. Not the escape. Not the precision with which the exit was planned.

I regret the casting.

I regret believing Dev's bitterness was aligned with mine. I wanted Raghav to bleed in the silence he built. And he did. Slowly. Publicly. With hashtags instead of handcuffs.

But Dev… Dev didn't destroy Raghav. He became him. Only more dangerous, because his affection was a mask, not a megaphone. He didn't execute the plan. He sanctified it. He took my outline and turned it into a myth—one where I wasn't the author, just the sacred symbol. He built me a shrine. Then nailed me to it.

*

Now I'm back. Not healed or broken. Just *aware.*

Freedom isn't stepping out of the cabin. It's erasing the narratives others write about you.

They called me a muse, a victim, a villain. But they were wrong. I'm none of those. I'm the woman who wrote the kill code.

*

So, did the plan fail?

It depends on who you ask.

If success means escape, yes. I escaped. If it means justice, yes, Raghav faced legal consequences.

But if it means control over the narrative? That's where the cracks showed.

The plan was flawless. The logistics were airtight. I had practised the lie until it became routine. I erased myself from digital maps. Swapped IDs. Rehearsed alibis. Even faked grief.

But what I didn't account for… was devotion.

Not from a man who loved me. From a man who wanted to possess the version of me that looked best under a spotlight.

I tried to destroy Raghav's brand. Instead, I became Dev's content. A flame lit to ruin one man, worshipped by another. I didn't just disappear. I became a performance. And he—Dev—became its curator.

*

And when I returned? There was no applause, just gossip.

Because in this story, there are no heroes. Only storytellers with blood on their keyboards.

*

Dev thought I was broken. Raghav thought I was back. The world thought I was healing.

But I was drafting. And like any good lawyer… I was building my closing argument.

He thought I came back for healing. But the truth? I came back because the plan was already in motion. I just needed proximity. To study him, to soften the public, to choose the day.

And when that day came? No one would suspect the woman who had once been kidnapped. Only the man who had been forgiven.

*

When the chaos settled, Raghav assumed I'd come back.

I didn't. I packed a small bag again, no fake notes this time. No goodbye.

The first time I left was impulsive. The second time was intentional. I left for Dehradun to my mother, alone, no cameras, no press, just me, my files, my freedom and just the door clicking shut behind me. Not because I was afraid. But because I couldn't live with a man who looked at my trauma like it was a shared blanket, something he could pull toward himself on colder days.

I didn't owe him proximity. Not anymore.

***

CHAPTER 7:
When An Apology Isn't Enough

"Some men apologise to heal. Others apologise to reset control. I had learned the difference."

Four Months.

That's how long it took for the bruises to settle in the marrow and the screaming to convert into silence. Not recovery—that's a word therapists sell in soft fonts and filtered captions. You don't recover from fire. You carry the scent. You walk into rooms, and someone recoils. Not from your words, but from the smoke leaking out of your breath.

*

Dehradun gave me three weeks of stillness I didn't trust. The silence didn't feel healing. It felt like an old hotel room waiting for a new crime.

The mornings came easily. Nights were harder, longer, quieter, filled with the echo of jokes that weren't funny anymore. My mother boiled milk too thick, like it could patch emotional corrosion. She never asked about Dev or Raghav. Or the disappearance that trended under #WifeInWithdrawal for six hours and thirty-seven seconds.

But one night, while folding a shawl that wasn't hers, she asked it: "Will you forgive him?"

I didn't answer. Forgiveness is a word stitched in soft thread and handed to women like a scarf in courtrooms. But mine was soaked, heavy. And no longer wearable.

*

The messages from Raghav started the same week. First, careful. Formal, like a client requesting an overdue document. "Checking in. No pressure. Just hope you're safe."

Then casual. "Thinking about dinner in Bandra. Remember that place with the awful chairs but great wine?"

Then personal. "I don't know how to undo the man I became, but I'm reading. Therapy. Podcasts. All the things broken men Google at 2 a.m."

And then finally, pathetic. "I don't deserve you. I'm not asking for a second chance. Just… less hate."

My mother read them. Pretended not to. Suggested I should at least reply. "If not for marriage," she said softly, "then for dignity."

Funny how dignity always feels like a compromise in a woman's mouth.

Today, at 3:02 a.m.: "Please don't make me a ghost in your story. I'm not asking for us. Just... Please… I don't want to be the villain in your story." The ghost wasn't him. It was me. I was the obituary he wrote for likes. He'd murdered me with satire, and now, it was my turn.

But I didn't need blood. I had something sharper: belief.

*

So, I returned. Quietly. No luggage. Just a thin cotton shawl over my shoulders, the same way widows wear grief without rings. Mumbai smelled the same. Hot concrete, diesel engines, jasmine oil in taxi upholstery, someone else's cigarette. The apartment smelled faintly of hope gone stale.

Raghav met me at the door like a man collecting a parcel he forgot he ordered. He didn't try to hug me, didn't reach for my hand. He stood like someone trying to remember the correct greeting for a language he never really spoke well. His face was thinner. Paler. Filtered grief and filtered light.

"Aarti... you came back."

Four words, zero accountability. No apology yet, because men like him think arrival *is* an apology.

I smiled. Clean. Precise. "I came back," I said, "to see if ghosts still shiver in this house."

*

He thought I came home for softness.

But softness is what men mistake for surrender. I came back for access. For scent trails. For metadata. Because revenge isn't just fire. It's a rehearsal. And no one rehearses better than women who've spent their entire lives being told to smile while bleeding.

Within hours, Raghav transitioned from predator to performance artist. He offered dinner the night I moved back in. Actually, not moved in, but the night I *appeared*. He called it "our second first date." I called it: *proof of stupidity*.

The table was too clean, the wine too room temperature. He wore a T-shirt that read *"Empathy is sexy"*. I stared at it like it was an unpaid bill.

"I'm glad you're back," he said, his voice trying to find its old rhythm, that scripted charm.

"I'm not," I replied, gently. "But I'm good at pretending."

He laughed. Of course he did. Men like him think candour is foreplay.

*

His guilt wore all the right costumes. He apologised in all the correct fonts: Times New Roman for *"Unlearning Myself"*,

Courier New in printed letters folded like guilt in half and Comic Sans—accidentally, insultingly—on a Post-it: *"You deserve softness. I'm trying."*

His guilt came gift-wrapped in quinoa bowls, burnt garlic, and lavender biscuits shaped like apology hearts. He signed up for therapy. Tagged me in posts with captions like: "Learning to sit in my own noise. #Healing." He cooked twice a week. He couldn't pronounce "rooibos," but he brewed it anyway.

Some nights, he left trays by my bedside: lukewarm chamomile tea, one broken biscuit, and a handwritten poem about regret written in the kind of handwriting men forget they practised in college notebooks before they discovered power was easier to buy than vulnerability.

It was sweet. And manipulative.

Because he didn't want forgiveness. He wanted a reaction. He wanted proof that his guilt was visible, that it was legible to the people watching from the sidelines. Even his apologies needed witnesses.

Guilt to him was theatre. To me, it was logistics. Just another spreadsheet, a new column added to the one labelled *Cost-Benefit Narrative Control.*

He did change. But not into a better man. He changed into a quieter man. Quieter isn't kinder. It's just fear in lowercase. He walked around like the floor was made of ice. Each step was tentative. Each sentence carried like a fragile glass of water: carefully balanced, overly polite.

"Hey, this isn't creepy. I promise," he said once, standing outside my room with a plate of toast shaped into a smiley face. He knocked twice, then waited too long before adding, "I just thought you might be hungry."

I took the plate. Closed the door. Heard him exhale, like I'd passed some unspoken test.

Another morning, I came down half-awake, bleary-eyed, still adjusting to the light. He reached out reflexively and brushed his lips against my temple—a soft, almost reverent kiss.

Then quickly added, "I hope this isn't too soon," like an actor anxious about reviews.

Later that week, he tried a joke while pouring herbal tea, something about Raghav's ego being more bloated than the ashram's lentil stew. I didn't laugh. I just looked at him.

He held the moment like a man holding his breath, then shrugged, too casual, eyes darting sideways. "Don't worry," he said with a sheepish smile. "You don't owe me a smile."

It was new, this performance of awareness, but it was still a performance. Even his growth needed applause.

"Do you see how much better I am?" he asked one night, voice soft, cracking under its own weight.

I smiled politely. Practised the social nod, the one you give relatives at weddings when they tell you you've lost weight, as if that's a compliment.

What I didn't say was the thing I had finally learned to think clearly: Yes. You've become predictable. And predictable men are easier to kill.

*

One morning, he left a flier next to my coffee mug: *Yoked: Where Love Finds Balance.* Couples' yoga. I could almost smell the copywriter's *chai* breath between the fonts.

"It'll be good for us," he said, running a hand through his unwashed hair like a man auditioning for emotional transparency. "Breathwork. Detox. Movement. Connection."

I raised an eyebrow. He smiled too widely. That nervous grin men wear when they're performing sincerity like a monologue they practised badly in rehearsal.

We went. Because fake harmony requires visibility.

Sanika, the instructor, had the kind of body that never held grudges. She smiled like a woman who had never been humiliated on camera. Her voice was soft, humid, always on the edge of a compliment.

"Let your hips open where your mouth won't," she said gently.

Raghav waved at her like they had gone to college together, or slept together, or maybe just imagined it the way men sometimes do with women in spandex. He always assumed familiarity before it was earned.

We unrolled our mats, front row. Proximity to performance. He leaned over, conspiratorial.

"If we get through this without suing each other," he whispered, "I'll consider us healed."

I reached for a foam block like it was a closing argument.

Cat. Cow. Downward Dog. Raghav grunted theatrically. Everyone laughed.

"You look elegant," he said. "I look like a man crawling out of karma debt."

And then, of course, the inevitable whisper, designed just for me, but loud enough for the people behind us to catch: "You could've warned me you're inflexible in yoga *and* marriage."

Laughter. Chuckles. The teacher smiled. Mistaking cruelty for charm is Mumbai's second favourite sport after cricket.

I smiled too. Adjusted my position. Memorised how long it would take a standard Clonazepam dosage to dissolve in tea. Counted backwards from twenty.

*

That night, he cooked *khichdi*. Added too much *ghee*. Oversteamed the broccoli until it looked like apologies boiled to death. "The body needs comfort after exertion," he said, offering the bowl like a communion wafer.

We sat across from each other like two people pretending to share a favourite movie when neither remembered the plot.

"You looked graceful today," he said, reaching for wine.

"You were loud," I said. "As usual."

He laughed, that old charming laugh, the one that sold out auditoriums when his career still belonged to him. "It's charm. You married charm."

I didn't flinch. "No," I said, my voice flat as a verdict. "I married a headline."

The spoon trembled in my hand—not from anger, not from fear, but from the truth pressing forward, heavy and unstoppable. What was the point of pretending anymore? Pretending we were cordial. Pretending love still lived here. Pretending there was anything left to salvage.

I wasn't here to sugarcoat. I was here to end the performance.

*

At night, as we lay in bed, his hand brushed against mine.

"I never realised I was a storm until you left," he confessed.. "But I'm learning. I'm quieter."

I nodded. Not because I agreed, but because I needed to remember the exact rhythm of his optimism.

"You feel safer now," he added, as if that was a compliment.

I almost laughed. Safer men don't keep scoreboards of women's reactions. Safer men don't gaslight with playlists and *chai*.

"I'm glad you feel that way," I said, turning to face him. My voice was like moonlight: soft, but sterile.

"You've changed too."

And he had. He had gone from predator to puppy. From bomb to brand ambassador for mindfulness. And that's what made him vulnerable.

Because predictability is the most dangerous trait a man like him can have.

*

Every morning after that was a performance.

He'd make oat milk lattes and call them intimacy. He'd mispronounce "*ashwagandha*" while quoting Brené Brown. He'd leave books by my bedside, titles like *The Body Keeps The Score* and *Attached*, as if literature could exonerate cruelty.

"Let's try again," he whispered one morning, handing me a bowl of cut fruit like it was a peace offering. I took it. I even kissed his forehead.

Because men trust touch more than truth. Because sometimes, survival looks like participation.

*

But beneath the routine, I was conducting an autopsy. Not on him, but on myself. What part of me had survived? What had calcified? What could be weaponised?

I logged everything. His new passwords, his blog drafts, his email drafts he hadn't sent yet, his mood swings and when they occurred and his voice notes to his therapist—yes, he backed them up in iCloud.

He had become open. Transparent. Accessible. And I? I had become air. Untraceable. Unsuspicious. The kind of woman men love when she's silent, soft, and unreal.

*

One night, I lay next to him like evidence under a white sheet. He tried to reach for me—not sexually, not even affectionately, just to *confirm* I was real.

I let him.

Because I needed to map his breath. Because I needed to time how long it took him to fall asleep. Because vengeance is best served spoon-fed: slow, bland, and in bed.

His fingers grazed my wrist, and he whispered, "I missed the way you smell."

I turned my face to the wall and imagined drowning in bleach.

Later that night, I found him slouched on the couch, head in his hands, the way men sit when the algorithm finally stops clapping.

"The last post didn't perform well," he muttered. "People think I'm faking it now. Like if I change, it's just marketing."

He was crying. Real crying. The kind that doesn't sell on reels because it looks too much like childhood shame. "I wanted to be better," he whispered. "I just didn't know how to stop needing the audience."

He looked up at me with wet lashes and raw breath like a boy who had just realised his father wasn't coming to his school play. "Aarti… what if I was broken before you? What if all of this… wasn't your fault?"

I stood there. Not angry. Not sympathetic. Just clinical. I watched the way a surgeon watches a patient describe the pain before opening the ribcage.

"You've been sorry for a long time," I said softly.

Then I walked into the kitchen, opened the fridge, counted the lavender biscuits left on the middle shelf, calculated the shelf life and estimated packaging disposal routes.

*

Remorse is not safety. Silence is not surrender. And men like Raghav? They're not tragic. They're *templates*.

He thought remorse made him safe. What he didn't know was that remorse is just repetition with better lighting. But all it did… was make him predictable. And predictable men? Predictable men aren't tragic. They're procedural. And procedural men? They're the easiest to kill.

*

By the third week, I knew two things: he would never truly change, and I no longer needed rage to win.

I only needed proximity, precision, and patience. And by now, I knew how he slept, what he dreamt about, what made him twitch. I had memorised his REM cycles the way scholars memorise poetry, not for beauty, but for power.

One night, I stood over him while he slept, the moonlight striping his face like prison bars.

He stirred. "What are you doing?" he mumbled.

"Just watching," I whispered.

And I was. I was watching the final act. Not murder. Just formatting.

Because death isn't always a weapon. Sometimes it's a draft. Scheduled, styled, and sent at just the right time.

***

PART *Two* THE INTELLECTUAL MURDER

CHAPTER 8:
Method Review

"You don't plan a murder. You write it like legislation—clause by clause, leak-proof, emotionless. Murder isn't drama. It's drafting."

3:17 a.m.

That's the hour when Mumbai stops pretending it's a city and reveals what it really is: machinery of the human kind. Endless metal softening into fatigue. The honks slow. Dogs curl up beneath unfinished scaffolds. The internet stops trying to sell you imported sneakers and starts whispering things you shouldn't ask but already knew you would.

And in the middle of it all is me. Awake, dry-eyed. Bent over spreadsheets in a room where the silence isn't restful—it's staged.

Down the hallway, Raghav was snoring again, nasal, arrogant, like his unconscious mind hadn't yet received the memo that humility was fashionable now.

I sat there under the shallow cone of my desk lamp, the rest of the flat sinking into dim neglect. My reflection in the glass of the window was thin, stretched by fatigue, familiar now in a way my body hadn't been to me in months. The walls weren't silent; they were complicit. Everything else was machinery: water coolers groaning in middle-class kitchens, ACs exhaling breath they couldn't afford to hold, and my fingers clicking across forensic PDFs with all the warmth of a guillotine designer.

I wasn't awake because of insomnia. I was awake because I had work to do. The kind that doesn't allow blinking.

I streamlined the mess of twenty tabs into one precise mission. The goal wasn't to find 'a way out'. The tabs were open: legal databases, journal archives, forensic reports written in exhausted academic English. The goal was to design the exit route: clean, clinical, unnoticed. Not incognito. I wasn't afraid of history anymore.

This wasn't curiosity. It was calibration.

I scrolled slowly, one knuckle balanced under my chin, the cursor blinking with the patience of someone folding funeral clothes. *Zolpidem toxicity, masked as fatigue. Quiet death signatures in forensic reports. Fatal interactions: diphenhydramine and alcohol metabolism. Quietest ways to die. Drug interactions that mimic fatigue. Respiratory depression without physical struggle. Common autopsy misses in India.* Every keystroke was intent without confession.

Case after case chronicled silent exits dressed in domesticity. 2024, Ahmedabad: Wife poisoned diabetic meds, blamed it on a sugar crash. 2025, Pune: Slow arsenic via herbal capsules. Delhi NCR: 'Blue drum' murder: wife vanished, husband's body in a water drum, missing for two months.

The methodology evolved, but the motive was eternal: escape without handcuffs.

I wasn't searching for *how to kill him.* I was searching for a way to kill without losing the trial. There's a difference.

Lawyers don't think like artists. Artists imagine revenge like a story. We don't imagine outcomes; we construct them, one clause at a time, with airtight alibis and calculated phrasing. We write endings like closing arguments before anyone else knows the trial has begun. I didn't need it to be violent. I didn't want violence. Violence stains. And stains are hard to explain in interviews.

What I wanted was silence. The kind that doesn't come with screaming or sirens. The kind that arrives gently, like steam lifting off lukewarm tea, unnoticed by anyone who wasn't taught to pay attention to things that don't scream for rescue. Murder wasn't the plan. *Absence* was. And like all elegant contracts, it would need revisions.

I opened a spreadsheet again. Not because I liked order, but because I respected it. The columns were brutal, precise, and clinical as old court exhibits. Methods. Advantages. Weaknesses. Outcome. Each row was a possibility I had already tested mentally and emotionally, in whispered research and old cases buried behind bar association subscriptions.

I tested each one like trial exhibits I'd studied in other people's ruined lives.

Method	**Pros**	**Cons**	**Verdict**
Drug Cocktail	Quiet	• Risk of vomiting • Toxicology red flags if autopsy is proactive	Too messy. Too traceable.
Drowning	Quick if staged	• Physical resistance • Postmortem bruising	Too intimate. I won't touch death.
Gas Leak	Passive	• Neighbours • Gas alarms, surveillance, nosy committees	Too public. Too residential.
Fall from Height	Public suicide staging	• Location-specific • CCTV timestamps, trajectory analysis	Cinematic? Yes. But this isn't a film.

Heart Attack Simulation	Clean in theory	• Requires prior cardiac condition • No predictable method of induction	Almost. And almost is prison.
Poison	Predictable in dosage	• Needs masking agent • Close monitoring post-dose • Vomiting ruins everything, especially carpets and plausible deniability	Possible, if calibrated.

I paused, feeling the dryness on my lips from the old turmeric tea he'd left for me earlier. Cooling now. Bitter. Like promises left in fridges too long.

That's when I realised: it didn't have to be one act. It could be an *accumulation*. Disguised as care. Served in steeped leaves and overcooked sincerity.

You don't kill a man like Raghav with violence. You kill him with confusion. The elegance of it made my throat ache with a kind of reluctant joy. I wasn't orchestrating a crime. I was designing an environment. Carefully, gently, like folding hospital corners on a bed you've already decided someone won't wake up in.

It wouldn't be a sudden thing. It would be gradual. Steeped, like over-brewed tea. First, he'd forget things; minor things, the details men blame on stress when their masculinity doesn't allow for anxiety. He'd call it exhaustion. I'd call it dosage.

I opened a new tab and named it *Project Silence*. Not because it ended sound, but because it ended his noise.

The Excel spreadsheet I had been curating for weeks. Columns so neat they could be mistaken for compassion. The cocktail was ordinary enough: clonazepam, diphenhydramine, melatonin. Innocent apart, symphonic together.

They wouldn't kill him. That wasn't the point. They'd dismantle him. They confuse time. Slow reflexes. Mute the will to argue. They make the body feel like it's betraying itself. First, his reflexes, then his memory, then his sentences: the punchlines would start to stumble, the sharpness would turn to static. The audience would drift away not because he was offensive, but because he wasn't interesting anymore.

He'll think it's stress, and I'll agree. "You're not sleeping well," I'll say. "Maybe see a doctor."

He won't. Because Raghav's version of masculinity never included check-ups. By the time it mattered, his body wouldn't fight. Why would it? His ambition would already be asleep. And ambition's the last organ to die. No dramatic resistance. Just the slow drift of a man whose muscles finally forgot what applause feels like.

And I would be there, brushing his hair back, quoting feminist essays to him like lullabies. Bell hooks with bedtime tea. Therapy quotes folded into porridge. Supportive. Loving. Quiet.

*

I'll log his symptoms, support his confusion, feed him hydration, and quote *bell hooks* quotes. And every day, I'll recalibrate him. Until the body he lives in becomes a stranger, until silence isn't just a mood: it's his resting heart rate, until the last time I handed him a glass of whisky, and it tasted like nothing. That's the trick about slow murder: they don't remember how alive tasted.

This isn't revenge. This is policy. Marriage had been the contract. His cruelty, the breach. This would be the termination protocol.

And when that night came, the night he slipped into that tub, the jazz spilling through speakers like melted candlelight, I wouldn't feel rage.

I didn't want blood. I wanted absence. The kind that makes people uncomfortable, not because someone screamed, but because *someone stopped talking*. Everything is on time. Everything organised. Everything inevitable. Because murder isn't madness. It's law school with better execution.

And when they ask me what happened, I'll say what all women learn to say eventually: "I don't know. I think... he just stopped."

And he will. Because policy isn't about justice. It's about completion. Clause by clause, leak-proof, emotionless.

At breakfast, Raghav's phone buzzed. "Google sent me a weird notification," he muttered. "Someone accessed my account at 3 a.m."

My chest tightened. My heartbeat quickened, loud enough that I feared it might give me away. I forced a smile, stirring his *chai* with the same hand that had deleted browser history only two hours ago. My fingers trembled just slightly against the spoon.

"Must be syncing errors," I said, shrugging like it was nothing.

He paused, eyes searching my face. Sweat gathered at the base of my neck. I slid a slice of papaya toward him, careful to disguise the dampness in my palm. He hesitated, then took it.

Trust is such fragile paper. Wet once, and it tears without warning.

***

CHAPTER 9:
The Murder Ledger

"If grief is chaos, revenge is curriculum. And I never failed a syllabus."

Some women collect memories. Some collect bruises. I collect patterns. And patterns don't lie.

Grief made me careful. Rage made me precise. Law made me invincible. I don't keep diaries. Diaries bleed. Diaries beg to be discovered. I keep ledgers that are clean, sharp and cold. Not for the emotions. For the numbers. The *proof.*

Because revenge isn't poetry. It's accounting. And this one needed balancing.

*

The file on my laptop was called *FinalTally.xlsx*. To anyone else, it looked like expense planning, productivity metrics. But between the formulas and colour-coded rows lived the slow reduction of Raghav Kapoor—writer, accidental activist, professional disappointment. Every row was a surrender, timestamped, clinical. Every dose, every twitch, every cognitive fracture framed as "healing fatigue," was colour-coded, clinical, and beautiful in its banality. Like death had a user manual. I didn't need fingerprints on murder weapons. I needed behaviour. Behaviour doesn't lie.

*

Day 6

It started small.

He forgot the Netflix password. I saw him hesitating for 3 seconds, and then he tried again. A flicker of embarrassment came upon his face, but was gone as quickly as it came.

"Wait… was it your birthday year or mine?"

He smiled and deflected. Blamed the update and laughed it off.

But I didn't. I stirred his tea, watched his fingers fumble at the keypad again, and logged it: *Forgetfulness Triggered. No Correction Applied.*

People don't notice the first forgetting. They call it tiredness. That's how rot begins: quietly, like damp creeping into drywall.

*

Day 9: First Shift

He stirred his tea counterclockwise. Raghav always stirred clockwise. That's how I knew the antihistamine was taking root; subtle, disorienting, just enough to tilt gravity under his rituals. *Motor Coordination Drift: Mild. Reaction Unconscious.*

He laughed at a podcast he hadn't even heard fully. I smiled back, refilled his cup, and upped the sedative by 0.25ml.

It had begun. The quiet dismantling.

*

Day 11: First Crack

He stood in front of the fridge for four minutes. Said he forgot why he opened it.

I told him, "You came for water."

He smiled gratefully like I had gifted him his own memory back. His gratitude made me nauseous. *Cognitive Pause Documented. Increased Dependency Response.*

"You're my anchor," he said that night. I didn't reply. I was already busy logging the dosage increase in the spreadsheet.

*

Day 15: The Pause

Day 15 brought hesitation.

Raghav woke up early. He brought me poorly brewed green tea and a trembling apology. "I… I forgot your birthday last year. You didn't even remind me."

His voice cracked, eyes unexpectedly wet. For a moment, my hand stilled over the ledger. Regret? Or a performance glitch? *Guilt Surge Detected. Memory Collapse Accelerated.*

I let the moment pass. A clinical deduction followed.

That night, I mixed in a pinch of powdered melatonin with his sleepy time tea, not enough to kill. Just enough to silence.

He used to be viral. Now he was dim. Blaming burnout. Stress. Pressure of public apologies.

Posting less. Tweeting poetry with spelling errors. Nobody noticed. The internet doesn't miss people. It just replaces them.

His audience drifted like fog, and I watched his vanity rot in real time.

*

Day 18: The Quiet Collapse

But I wasn't seeing burnout. I was watching scheduled decay.

He stared at a doorknob for thirty seconds before realising the door was already open. "It's the weather," he mumbled.

"Or your nervous system," I replied, folding laundry.

He chuckled. "Always so dark."

No, darling. Just always correct.

By the time he confessed that he couldn't remember if he sent an email or just thought about it hard enough, I knew I was close. I wasn't poisoning him. I wasn't murdering him. I was narrating his disappearance, sentence by sentence, like an editor revising a book no one really wanted to finish reading anyway. The law had taught me one thing better than justice: control the language, and you control the trial. Facts don't win cases. Stories do. I didn't need a motive. I needed framing.

That night, I added a new field: *Confusion vs. Comprehension Ratio.* I created a formula to track *how often he agreed to things he didn't fully hear.* It was at 62%. Progress.

*

Day 21: External Ripples

Raghav's friend, Krish, visited.

"Bro, you're zoning out," Krish said, half-laughing, half-concerned. "You called me at 2 a.m. asking about a TED talk we attended… last year."

Raghav laughed it off, but Krish's eyes lingered. *External observation triggered. Risk flagged.*

I neutralised it at dinner. "You've been forgetting things," I said softly. "I think you need to rest."

He nodded too quickly.

*

Day 22: Suspicion

On Day Twenty-Two, he hesitated at the tea.

He paused mid-sip and furrowed his brow. "Did you change the honey?"

I didn't flinch. Only amateurs panic at flickers. "No," I lied. "You just haven't tasted it properly since the cold."

He nodded, still unsure, but still sipping. "Guess I'm just being paranoid," he finally muttered, and continued sipping.

Those ten seconds taught me more about survival than two decades of legal training. Murder isn't about hiding intent. It's about hiding precision. Precision gives you away. Sloppiness forgives.

I added it to the ledger. Paranoia pinged. Control restored.

*

That night, I stood over his sleeping body. Not with rage or regret. Just silence. The kind that doesn't want justice. The kind that wants completion.

"I'm sorry you've slept next to that all these years," he said, half-asleep, half-hoping I would forget the sentence in the morning.

"You've been snoring since day one," I replied. "You're just hearing yourself now."

I stood, kissed the top of his head the way widows-to-be do when they know the obituary photo has already been selected, then walked to my study, opened the spreadsheet, and logged the event. I increased the antihistamine dosage by 1 ml. Not for safety, but for symbolism.

*

By Day 26, his fingers trembled buttoning shirts, his phone turned up in the freezer, and he cried in the shower, thinking I couldn't hear, the ledger had no doubts left.

On Day 28, the narrative was established. 'Tech Burnout' Confirmed. Medical Suspicion Deflected.

Dr. Khatri lived two floors below. Retired. Diabetic. Widow-softened. Still believed medicine was more conversation than code. Raghav called him *"Uncle."* I called him *"a liability-free medical stamp with nostalgia for ethics."*

The elevator ride was short, but perfectly timed. It was morning, my hair was unbrushed, and my eyes were smudged. A look curated like courtroom evidence, labelled *fatigued but functioning.*

I sighed. Just loud enough. "He's not sleeping much. Keeps forgetting things. Yesterday, he asked if we'd had lunch. . . twice."

Dr. Khatri frowned. The kind of frown that diagnoses without investigating. "You've been pale, *beta*. Mood swings?" he asked, examining Raghav casually.

I smiled, weary. "Too much screen time. He's detoxing."

Khatri nodded approvingly. "Tech burnout. Happens all the time. Overstimulation. He needs rest, not prescriptions."

Exactly.

I nodded with soft gratitude, the kind women use when asking for nothing but getting everything. He stepped out onto his floor. I typed the note as the elevator climbed.

*

Day 32: Final Calibration

I swapped his sleep tea for plain water. Left the pills untaken. There was no change in behaviour. The body was dependent. The mind was a slow-drip collapse.

Autonomy compromised: 84%

That's how stories are built. Not with lies, but with trusted men and women who know exactly when to look tired.

*

The Confirmation Test

I added a nonsense line to a newspaper headline: *"Mumbai considers compulsory whale adoption."*

He quoted it back at brunch. Didn't realise whales weren't residents.

Critical reasoning: Suspended. Final escalation approved.

*

That night, I deleted the last photo of us. Anniversary dinner, his arm possessively around my shoulder, me already tilting away. Trash. Empty bin. No backups. I didn't murder him. I erased his essence. Logged it, tracked it, archived it.

When he would be found—empty-eyed, forgotten by his own body—I wouldn't need alibis. I'd have receipts. Receipts no court would bother to read.

I wasn't seeking closure. I was writing *clarity*. No violence. No mess. No blood on the tiles. Just a ledger. A woman with too much memory. And a man who finally became forgettable.

They'll say it was stress, or heartbreak, or grief fatigue. They'll blame burnout, or post-feminist guilt, or digital noise. They'll say everything, except the truth.

That the woman who loved him kept a spreadsheet. And in that spreadsheet, she made silence permanent.

***

CHAPTER 10:
The Ledger Gets Another Row

"He mistook survival for reconciliation. I mistook it for research."

I remember the night he cried. It wasn't the first time I'd seen him cry. But this was different.

Not the shallow sniffles men perform when they've been caught lying, or the single tear slipped out for Instagram-worthy regret. No. This was ugly. Snot, shaking hands, a body curled like it didn't know what else to be except guilty.

It was so raw, I almost didn't recognise him. And for the briefest moment, five seconds, if I'm being generous, I forgot the spreadsheet. I forgot the yoga trap. I forgot the warm chamomile tea laced with 0.25 mg of clarity and the note I had already titled *Eulogy for the Emotionally Literate.*

For five seconds, I saw a man breaking.

And I asked myself the most dangerous question a broken woman can ever ask: *What if this time, he means it?*

But truth doesn't arrive in breakdowns. It arrives in behaviour. And behaviour, in men like Raghav, has always been strategic.

So, I brewed another cup of tea.

The next morning, he brought me honey-lemon tea, lukewarm, bitter at the back of the tongue. "You okay?" he asked, voice soft, eyes not. He held the cup a second too long, sniffing for betrayal. "I didn't sleep well," I said, brushing a hand through my hair with a perfectly curated sigh. "Too much honesty."

He chuckled. The way men do when they believe your sarcasm is just wit and not war. He kissed my temple and left. I counted the steps. Twelve to the door. Another six to his desk. And when the door clicked behind him, I opened the laptop. No lights, no sounds. Just the fluorescent hum of the machine and the steady pulse of my own heartbeat, measured now in plans instead of panic.

The spreadsheet blinked back at me like a guilty accomplice: faithful, clinical, ruthless. It welcomed me the way familiar weapons welcome soldiers who've finally stopped pretending they'll take up gardening instead.

I opened a new tab. This one wouldn't be financial. This one would be anatomical. Typed the title: *Somatic Decline Schedule.*

Not dramatic. Not violent. Elegant.

Because fake domesticity was burning calories I didn't owe anyone. If I was going to maintain the theatre, I needed a timeline. Not just a motive. Not just means. A *schedule.* Quiet. Precise. Elegant. The kind of plan that doesn't arrive with sirens but slips through an unlocked bathroom door like steam curling around someone who trusted too easily.

Revenge is not always fire. Sometimes, it's a slowly closing door. One hinge at a time. One unspoken line. One spoon of turmeric latte too bitter to question.

*

He started forgetting things. At first, it was charming. Like a man trying too hard to pretend he wasn't always in control.

"Did I tell you I donated to that gender violence NGO?" No, Raghav. You told the internet. You tagged me. You posted it with #FeministHusband.

Then: "Have we already had this conversation?" Yes. Twice. But I nodded like a woman who understood trauma and not manipulation.

Later, I found him staring at the stove like he had forgotten how fire worked. "I think I'm tired," he mumbled. "Like, soul-tired."

Perfect.

I noted the changes. Not like a partner. Like an archivist. Like a widow counting the seconds between a heartbeat and the echo.

His wellness routine became a stage. Ayurvedic detox, moonstone bracelets, deep-breathing with influencers who pronounce "trauma" like a hashtag. He suggested we renew our vows. Somewhere barefoot. In Bali. On a beach where healing retreats serve smoothies named after goddess archetypes. He said we should get tattoos. He said I was glowing.

I said I was exfoliating grief. He believed it.

*

That night, while he snored through a motivational podcast on his laptop, I accessed his private journal folder. Raghav had always kept notes for his 'redemption memoir'.

I edited them, line by line. Inserted phrases like: *"Lately, I don't trust my own mind,""It's exhausting pretending to heal when I'm eroding,""I hope Aarti forgives me… even if I never forgive myself,"* *"I don't know how to be a man without applause,"* *"She didn't destroy me. She just finally left the script I wrote for her,"* *"If I disappear, tell them it wasn't her. Tell them it was silence that did it."*

His words, dressed in despair, timestamped authentically, waiting for discovery by whichever investigator trawled through his digital leftovers. Not framing. Planting inevitability.

I left them there. For later.

*

One evening, while slicing cucumbers, he kissed my forehead. The air was too still, too staged; his hands lingered, too soft, like he had watched a tutorial on intimacy and wanted to see if he could get it right this time.

"You're quieter," he said. "I like this version of you."

I dried my hands. Placed the knife down. Turned. Looked at him like a priest might look at a confessor, too late in the appointment to finish the ritual. "You just never learned to hear the silence," I said.

His lips parted like he wanted to say something profound. He settled for a smile. I returned it, one beat too late. He didn't notice.

*

It's funny how easily he let me back in. As if survival were a trust exercise. As if the woman who vanished and returned without bruises was somehow softer. He forgot, but I didn't.

Every toothbrush he bought was in pastel colours. Every book he left by my bed: *Daring Greatly*, *The Four Agreements*, *Why Men Cry (and why it's not enough)*. Each was a post-it in my dossier. Every night, I logged Melatonin dosages, supplements taken, cognitive lapses observed and mood fluctuation vs. apology frequency.

He became the subject. I became the author.

And I had learned now: Men like Raghav don't fear blood. They fear silence. They fear indifference dressed in intimacy. They fear a woman who doesn't flinch when they cry.

*

One evening, as we scrolled through Netflix suggestions, he turned to me. "You know… I feel lighter these days."

I nodded gently. "You're fading," I whispered in my head.

He smiled again. He thought I meant love. I meant the ledger. Row by row, the old story was dissolving. No climax, no crime. Just… omission.

Because some women stab with scissors. Others rewrite the will.

That night, I deleted the backup folder titled *"Moments with Aarti"* from his hard drive. Gone were vacation selfies, anniversary post drafts, and curated Instagram captions. Erased not because they pained me, but because they anchored him.

*

He'd be archived like bad code, like a recalled product, like a blog that once joked about death and ended up teaching someone how to do it without fingerprints.

Not with rage, not with poison. Just… formatting.

***

CHAPTER 11:
Rehearsing Widowhood

"They say grief can't be faked. They've clearly never met a woman who's had to survive it on camera."

It began like everything else in this city: under fluorescent lights, alone, half-drunk tea curling cold in chipped ceramic, algorithms muttering softly like late-night confessions. Grief wasn't new to me. Its performance was.

I wasn't watching Netflix anymore. I was on YouTube, dissecting footage like a pathologist with emotional cadavers. I spent my evenings studying women like archaeologists study fragments of older civilisations, piecing together the facial grammar of mourning. Widows, yes. Some raw, collapsed, mascara curling downward like their spines. Some polished grief in black silk, grief with contouring, grief with publicists. The ones who went viral did both. Collapse with posture. Fragility with market awareness. Just enough sorrow to soften the frame. Just enough dignity to keep the men in the comments saying things like *"She's so strong,"* while the other half muttered *"Sociopath."*

I watched them blink. I watched them break. I bookmarked the ones that knew how to let the tear fall at the exact moment the interviewer asked, "What will you miss most?" I need the algorithm to believe me when the time comes.

One woman in particular: Delhi, a political wife, pearl earrings, no lipstick, said softly, *"I still listen for his slippers in the hall."* I played it back three times. Not for meaning. For tempo. This wasn't empathy. This was choreography.

I wasn't studying grief. I was studying its performance *vocabulary*. Because mourning, like everything else women are allowed to feel, has been monetised. Grief is PR. And women only get sympathy if they mourn *beautifully*.

I set up the front camera of my phone. Collarbone framing. Widow angles. Hair imperfect enough to signal collapse, neat enough to whisper dignity. Indian widows don't wail. Not anymore. They hold it in the posture of their shoulders, the clean break in a sentence, the slight quiver at the wrong word, *accidental, but rehearsed.*

I mimicked her hand, loosely holding a tissue, as if grief wasn't allowed to grip too tightly. I blinked. Once. Twice. Practised the downward glance, not all the way, just slightly off-centre. Enough to look private, enough to look caught.

I hit record. Too dry.

Replay. Critique. Eyes moved too soon.

Replay. A smile crept in. Redo.

Nothing is more traitorous than a smile slipping out while practising heartbreak.

I adjusted my posture, angled my head to the right. Because mourning looks better in profile.

Hit record again.

The first tear landed too soon. I wiped it away, irritated. Not because it was fake, but because it was poorly timed. The rehearsal had to be flawless. Not the dramatic breakdown you see in courtroom dramas. No. The kind of grief that earns sympathy without suspicion. The kind that survives CCTV footage, police reports, and neighbourhood gossip threads.

I deleted the video. I clicked 'record' on my phone. Gaze downward. Inhale softly.

"He…he wasn't supposed to…" I trailed off, a tremor building at the edge of my jaw. Pause. Blink three times, let one tear streak. Tilt head slightly, draw breath as though drowning in disbelief.

But when I replayed the video, my fingers clenched. Too calculated. Delete.

*

Try again. This time, half-whisper: "He's… he's gone." Let the voice catch, blink rapidly, turn slightly away from the lens, like it were too painful to look at my own reflection.

Better. Almost believable.

I adjusted the camera angle.

*

Then, rustling.

My ears snapped towards the sound of the main door. I hurriedly wiped my cheek, yanked my phone off its stand. The maid, Leela, appeared in the doorway, frowning, her mop bucket in hand.

"Madam… you, okay?" Her eyes darted from the mirror to my damp cheeks.

A pause. The longest three seconds of the week.

I forced a brittle laugh. "Old video… memory of my father. Anniversary tomorrow," I lied, voice steady but strained. A lie rehearsed for moments like this.

Leela hovered, unsure, then nodded. "Okay, madam… you looked… upset… just checking."

As she left, I pressed my back against the cold wall, heartbeat loud in my throat. Note to self: Lock the door during rehearsals.

*

Later that day, I opened Raghav's old journals.

He hadn't touched them in weeks. I flipped through, stopping at blank pages, and started writing in his style. Melancholic, self-critical, vaguely remorseful. *"I think I've done too much damage to be fixed," "She deserves a man who remembers anniversaries, not someone who forgets birthdays," "If anything happens, it's exhaustion… not her fault. She stayed."*

The perfect breadcrumb trail for any future discovery.

In the bathroom, I watched myself in the mirror again. This time, without the phone. Just me, no camera, no witness. And yet… I cried. One tear, perfectly timed. I clicked 'record' on my phone. This time, I didn't say anything. Just blinked. Let the breath flutter like it might be interrupted by something unspeakable.

Then I said it. Quiet. Raw. Like it hurt to say. Like it burned on the way out. "He didn't deserve this."

Pause. One tear. Precise. Clean. It dropped along my cheek like punctuation. Beautiful in that way that pain sometimes is when it doesn't yet smell like rot.

I hit save. I didn't need it yet. But I would. And I'd be ready.

I remembered sitting in a therapist's office two years ago, when the miscarriage was still fresh, when the house still smelled of antiseptic and my mother's grief steaming from kitchen burners. The therapist, all soft cardigans and beige intentions, had asked, *"Why do you think you don't allow yourself to cry?"*

I didn't answer.

I didn't cry at my wedding. Not when my father gripped my wrist like property changing hands. Not when the guests called my quietness elegant. Not during the blood on the bathroom tile. Not when Dev's fingerprints bruised the soft insides of my elbows like unspoken questions.

I didn't cry because crying was currency, and I don't spend unless I need change.

Now, years later, in this dim Mumbai apartment, I sat in front of the mirror, no makeup, no safety nets, just my own breath fogging up the frame. I blinked. Tilted. And when the tear came, I let it. On cue. Controlled. Measured. A single perfect descent, like a punctuation on the closing of an argument.

He didn't deserve this. And I meant it. Not the way the internet would think.

He didn't deserve a soft ending. He didn't deserve peace. He deserved discomfort, questions, and the public doubting whether he was ever really as charming as his tweets implied. But what he would get was mercy. Because *I* understood legacy. And cruelty is remembered longer than pity.

There would be three versions of the story when the time came. I rehearsed them in variations, like trial exhibits: One whispered. One broken. One elegant. The Whispered, broken breath: "He didn't deserve this." *(Private camera. For morning news reels.)* Said softly, slight head tilt: "He didn't deserve this." *(For evening interviews with panellists who quote Rumi.)* Spoken into the mirror, pause, glance down: "He didn't… deserve this."

(For myself. When I need to believe I've done the necessary.)

I could almost see the headlines forming: crisp fonts, clickbait tones, keywords optimised for outrage and sympathy. *Tragic wife. Brave widow. Mysterious survivor.* Each one was crafted like a press kit persona, tailored for a different media outlet. Each one flattened me into something marketable. Whichever version the world decided they liked best, I'd give them. People don't actually care about the truth. They care about *cohesion.* Give them a line they can hold like prayer beads. I'll provide the prayer.

I wasn't mourning. I was in costume. And grief is just costume design with better lighting.

Two weeks. That's what the ledger said. His deterioration would reach the necessary softness by then. No obvious illness.

Just exhaustion. Emotional strain. The kind of death that men slip into after too many months pretending they know how to repair themselves, but running out of applause before they can finish.

I'd stay. Not as the wife. As the widow-in-waiting.

I'd watch him take the last sip—count the seconds, not breaths. I'd note the flush in his cheeks, the droop in his eyelids, the precise moment silence stopped being an emotion and became a symptom.

I wouldn't flinch when he collapsed. I would wait.

When the maid found him, the tea would still be warm on the table. Jasmine curling through the apartment like a perfume someone chose with careful nostalgia. Coltrane low in the background, that saxophone drifting like silk just slightly out of tune.

I'd stand in the hallway. Barefoot, like an old myth, eyes puffy, mouth slightly parted, tissue in hand. Not screaming. Screaming's vulgar. I'd tremble. I will gasp once. Just tremble. Just enough to satisfy middle-class hysteria, but restrained. Grief that could pass in print without smudging ink.

Then: "He's not breathing." The words rehearsed so well that they didn't even feel like acting anymore. Because that's the trick of well-performed grief. It's not that you forget it's a lie. It's that you start believing the grief itself deserves to be true, even if the reason for it was never love, only narrative necessity.

I wasn't born knowing how to mourn. I taught myself. And now? When the time came, I wouldn't just mourn. I would perform. And the world would clap.

***

CHAPTER 12:
Trial Run

"Sometimes the best alibi isn't your innocence—it's your invisibility."

1:11 a.m. Palindrome time. Symmetry. The kind of number that makes anxious people believe in patterns. I don't believe in luck anymore. I believe in rehearsals.

The apartment was mine that night. Not by affection, not by inheritance, not even by right. But by function, by usage and by *intent.* Emotional occupancy had expired in that house years ago. But tactical occupancy? That was different. That was practical. That was the law.

Raghav was in Karjat. A yoga retreat with filtered water and overpriced detox teas. He'd sent a photo earlier that evening, shirtless, glowing, copper tumbler in hand. His chest still bore the arrogance of someone who thought sunlit wellness could fix old cruelty. The caption read: *Healing my gut. And my guilt.*

I didn't reply. Just turned off read receipts. The modern version of unfinished violence.

The house was mine tonight. Not emotionally—it hadn't been in years—but tactically. That's what mattered. I moved with the efficiency of someone who's cleaned up worse: miscarriages, broken promises, bruises disguised as weekend mishaps. My hands knew the rhythm. My lungs knew the pacing.

Tonight was a dress rehearsal. No improvisation. No adrenaline. Just the precise violence of narrative. The USB was blank, of course. A prop. The kind of clue idiots find and congratulate themselves for discovering. I snapped it clean with pliers—rusty ones, not because I needed rust but because fingerprints don't adhere as well to neglected tools. I dropped it behind the study desk. Not hidden. Not displayed. Just placed. The kind of detail lazy men miss and tired women find and decide not to report. Clues don't solve crimes. They just keep people busy.

Then I chose the vase. Blue ceramic. Not expensive. Gifted by one of Raghav's self-consciously spiritual friends, someone who called furniture "pieces" and described salad as an aesthetic. Raghav had once called it "soulless decor," and I'd agreed, not because I cared, but because I knew I would one day break it. It shattered against the floor like something polite being told it was no longer needed.

Shards were scattered across the tile with a kind of reluctant honesty, like they knew they weren't part of a real crime but wanted to behave respectfully anyway. The laptop glowed in the dark like an accomplice.

I deleted the safe folders: files too mundane to matter, but important enough to be noticeable. *"Legal Notes," "Client Drafts,"* and one innocently labelled *"Tax Projections."* Just enough erosion to seed confusion, not investigation.

I wiped browser trails, disabled auto-backups, and cleared my secondary phone history. Except… one planted search remained, faint enough to be an accident: *"exhaustion and memory loss husband help forums."*

Deleting is not about erasure. It's about narrative erosion. You don't stage chaos. You stage an *absence.* Absence of meaning. Absence of control. Absence of explanations that don't quite make sense, but not enough to look fake. A woman missing her paperwork? Boring. Forgettable. Believable.

I left the front door ajar. Not wide open. That's theatre. That's amateur. I left it just unsettled, slightly pushed inward, enough to be noticed, but not enough to invite heroics. Fear doesn't kick open doors. It leaves them unsettled, the way someone does when they don't know whether they're being followed or just imagining the footsteps.

Then I stood there for a moment, feeling the soft hum of the refrigerator behind me, the faint citrus of the floor cleaner someone forgot to rinse properly in the corners of the kitchen, the smell of printer ink still lingering from the last page I didn't bother filing away.

And I picked up the phone, dialled the local police station. The voice I used wasn't panicked. Panic is the noise women are taught to make when they want protection but know they won't receive it.

"Hello?" My voice was soft, controlled. With just enough tremble to echo through protocol. "Hello… yes… I think someone's been inside… no, nothing taken… but I don't… I don't feel safe."

Two deliberate pauses. Controlled inhale. That pause was the most important note in the whole performance. Hysteria gets dismissed. But fear, neatly arranged, commands attention. Silence with fracture earns a procedure. I didn't want protection. I wanted paperwork.

The constable arrived forty-eight minutes later, smelling faintly of betel nut and resentment. Five foot six, with circles under his eyes deep enough to store case files. His shoulders slumped like they'd given up asking for promotions. The belt hung loose on his waist, and his uniform clung to him like someone else's regret, poorly fitted and long since unchosen. He said "Madam" four times in the first two minutes. Always softly. As if reminding himself that I wasn't going to be the story he wanted tonight. He didn't look for fingerprints. Didn't ask about motives. Didn't even notice the ceramic dust under my heel.

"What's missing, Madam?" he asked, not because he cared, but because it was the script he was paid to perform.

I nodded, fragile but not dramatic. Not helpless. Just *unsteady*. The kind of steady that makes tired men nervous because they know that strength costs them paperwork. "Just... files," I murmured. "Client files."

He wrote it down slowly. Non-criminal disturbance. No visible theft. Minor scene damage. "Might be a prank. You said the door was open?"

He doesn't write this as a break-in. He writes it like a warning. A nudge to be more careful next time. It was a suggestion. That's how women disappear in this country: not in violence, but in clerical errors. His pen scratched slowly across the paper. No notes about the USB.

No mention of how the lock wasn't broken, just left vulnerable. He never asked what was on the USB. Never touched the laptop. Didn't even notice the ceramic dust under my slipper. He told me to lock my doors and call again if it happens.

I signed the report with shaky fingers and a fragile smile. Then he left without a second glance. I watched the curve of his back as he walked away.

And when I closed the door behind him, I made sure the click was audible. The punctuation of responsibility, punctuated by cheap deadbolts and the memory of borrowed keys.

The next morning, the report arrived via courier. Thin envelope. Cheap paper. Filed under: *"Non-criminal disturbance, no visible theft, minor scene damage."* Filed like something you throw away before breakfast. That phrasing will come back. I sat with that report for a long time, running my fingers along its edges, the way someone might trace the edge of a sleeping lover's jaw.

I folded it in half. Then in half again. Then tucked it under the tray on my desk, the one labelled *Pending Correspondence*, because that's what it was now: a pending performance.

This was the rehearsal. The dry run. The trial run wasn't about getting caught. It was about seeing how easy it was to *not* be questioned.

*

Police don't pursue still women. They pursue violence, blood, men with weapons, and stories that can be condensed into a soundbite. A missing document doesn't get an investigator. A missing pulse does.

I opened the real notebook next. Not the spreadsheets. Not the ledger. The one Raghav never knew about. The one that didn't track dosages or symptoms, but *methods of presence.* The subtle art of being *the right kind of broken* at the right time.

At the top of the page, I wrote: "For the real crime, never perform fear. Fear invites suspicion. Perform sorrow. Sorrow is unimpeachable." Fear makes them look at the scene. Sorrow makes them look at you.

The trial run was over. Next time, there won't be a rehearsal. Only silence and a flawless crime scene. You don't hide the crime. You hide yourself. The perfect crime isn't one that goes unnoticed; it's the one that never feels worth noticing.

***

CHAPTER 13:
The Dinner Before Death

"Some people poison relationships slowly. I just took it to its logical conclusion."

The table looked exactly like it used to back when we pretended to be people who liked each other. Linen white enough to suggest innocence. Candles with just enough flicker to pass for warmth. Plates cantered with geometric cruelty: symmetrical, calculated, dead-eyed. There was no centrepiece. Just space. Absence, framed.

Outside, the latemonsoon sky rolled thunder across Mumbai's rooftops, a percussion fit for executions. Neon leaked through rain-glazed windows, bathing the room in a lurid pulse: red, blue, violet, like police lights practising.

I layered the soundtrack with intent: Chet Baker, yes, but played through an old gramophone so every trumpet breath arrived scratched and imperfect, like lungs that had loved too hard. I lit a lavendersoy candle for olfactory misdirection; memory confuses tranquillity with safety, and I needed him sedated by nostalgia.

I'd made *masoor dal.* His favourite. Clove, cinnamon, nostalgia weaponised. The smell of Sunday afternoons when homework was undone, and guilt hadn't yet become a marital language. He once said it tasted like happiness before obligation. Tonight, it tasted like rehearsal.

Everything was *almost* romantic in the same way abandoned amusement parks are *almost* cheerful. Familiar, but off. A little *too* still. I'd even ironed the napkins. The white ones. The ones we bought when we thought marriage meant hosting, not performing. Folded them like apologies. Crisp. Lifeless.

The wine waited.

*

He entered barefoot, vulnerable, that damn *kurta* on jeans wrinkled in just the right places to signal he was *trying*. His face still held the echo of a boy who once believed being broken made him more lovable. And for a heartbeat—just one—something in me softened. Not forgiveness. Just recognition.

There he was, the man I'd once fought for at dinner tables, defended in bad times, believed could be more than the sum of his clever lines. He looked… endearing. Exhausted in a way that made him look younger. Almost human.

But then he hesitated at the doorway, the hesitation of a man who senses something unscripted, but walks in anyway. He always had terrible instincts.

"*Dal*?" His voice cracked slightly, confusion rounding his features.

I smiled like a woman welcoming back a husband from a war that only one of them fought. "Felt like home food."

He pulled out the chair but didn't sit immediately. That old Raghav hesitation, like he was waiting for a punchline that never came. He touched the wine bottle, glanced at the plates, and the candle I lit more out of habit than romance.

"This… smells nice."

"It's dinner," I replied flatly.

"I've been thinking," he said. "About everything."

Of course, you have. Guilt has a ticking clock.

"I wasn't fair to you."

"No," I said. "You weren't." And I let that sentence hang, like a noose waiting for gravity.

He picked at his food, slow, reverent, as if each bite might absolve him. "This… tastes like home," he whispered.

"It is," I said, and smiled again. But I meant the final home. The one without a return address.

*

He poured the wine himself this time. A small miracle. He'd always waited for things: dinner, forgiveness, affection, as though being male entitled him to them without request.

"To us?" he said, glass raised.

"To the in-between," I offered.

He laughed that soft chuckle he used when he didn't understand but didn't want to admit it. He drank. But not deeply enough.

*

I watched his throat as he swallowed. I watched the slow descent of liquid and pride. I watched the hope in his eyes rise just a little too fast. Not yet. The moment wasn't ripe. This was foreplay. Murder, when done right, isn't sudden. It's a conversation.

"I wrote something," he said, suddenly. "This week. A poem." He reached into his pocket. Pulled out a folded page. Shaky hands. Theatre hands.

"You don't have to—"

But he was already reading. It was clumsy. Sentimental. Rhymes that didn't land. Metaphors that sounded like they belonged in refrigerator magnets. But then, that line. That one line.

"You held my silence like it was sacred, even when it became your sentence."

My fork hesitated mid-air. And for a second, not long, not forgiving, not weak, just a flicker of an old organ twitching inside me, I felt *seen*. By the very man who spent years looking right through me.

This was not in the plan. He wasn't supposed to sound human tonight. Not when I'd spent weeks recalibrating him into background noise. For a flash of a second, I considered clearing the table and calling it off. What if this was the turning point? What if this version, fragile, humbled, was the one I wanted all along?

Then I remembered every apology that had been bookmarked but never finished. Every night spent practising invisibility while he trended on the internet for clever lines crafted from my humiliation.

No. Not again.

The nausea wasn't guilt. It was *recognition*. I swallowed it like I'd swallowed everything else for years: promises, disappointments, backhanded compliments that wore cologne.

"That's… something," I said. And left it there. Praise is too intimate to be wasted on ghosts.

*

We ate in almost-silence. His movements slowed; not from poison, but from reflection. Which, on him, looked like regret trying to dress itself in a tuxedo. But the doubt scratched harder when he put down his spoon halfway.

"I... I don't know why… I'm just not hungry," he muttered, pushing the plate aside.

My stomach twisted. Fewer bites. Slower effect. Unpredictable absorption. A variable I hadn't accounted for.

"You barely ate," I said, quieter than intended.

He shrugged, a small, pathetic motion. "Wine's enough."

No, it wasn't. Not for the dosage calibrated in the spreadsheet hidden two folders deep under innocuous work files. My throat tightened. Should I nudge him to finish? Press guilt? Or let the night drift, uncertain?

He stood, running a hand through his hair. "I'll shower… might help."

I smiled. A soft, practised smile, the kind that doesn't reach the eyes.

"Go ahead."

*

When he finally stood to leave the table, he touched my shoulder gently. A ghost of intimacy. Like a man brushing past his own death but not recognising the scent.

I kept my expression steady, pushed the wine bottle to the side. I checked the quantity left: close to two-thirds gone. Not ideal. But workable. Every muscle in my body pushed for recalculation, recalibration. No poison tonight. Slow symptoms. Delayed disorientation. Mild confusion by morning.

Fine.

I pivoted. He walked away, not knowing that each step he took was a countdown, not knowing that the book on his bedside table, the one he never finished, would remain forever bookmarked on the last night he existed as a husband.

*

The living room needed to look mundane, lived-in, not staged.

I unbuttoned the top two buttons of my *kurta*, let my hair loosen into something resembling comfort. I shut off the gramophone, and the trumpet died mid-sigh. I returned to the table with gloved fingers and cleared the table. Every spoon, every plate, every trace of the evening. I refolded the poem. Not for memory. For *evidence.* A snapshot of the man who almost said the right thing before I erased him.

The wineglass still held a fingerprint. I didn't wipe it. Let it be his last signature.

I blew out the candle. Lavender smoke coiled upward, slow, soft, unbothered. Like a soul forgetting where it came from.

*

The house fell quiet, but not peaceful. Peace is something you earn. This silence? This was the stillness before the storm, the inhale before the scream. And I never missed my cue.

From the bathroom, water ran, his off-key humming barely audible through the door. I allowed myself one last hesitation. I stood in the doorway, clutching a damp dishcloth, eyes closed. What if this were forgivable? What if I could just… leave?

But the answer was the same; it had always been. He'd heal just enough to break me again.

*

A voice whispered inside me, the soft, deadly reminder: "Tonight isn't about ending him. It's about ending the repetition."

Then, I decided to finish it.

And like every story Raghav crafted to glorify himself, he miscast the author. I was always the pen, the ink, and the hand that pressed too hard.

***

CHAPTER 14:
The Night the Jazz Went Flat

"Drafts become final not when you finish writing, but when you stop revising."

Hallway lights in our Powai highrise run on motion sensors: sterile LEDs that flare awake when they detect presence, then fade, bored, if you stand too still. I choreographed my steps to their rhythm; each flicker was my curtain cue, each dimming my invisibility cloak.

Step one: wave at the darkness; let the strip of light bloom.

Step two: slip the small brown vial of Brotx91's vicious sibling into the pocket of my silk robe.

Step three: wait until the light begins its slow fade.

Step four: move again, so it resurrects.

The corridor learned my rhythm the way prisoners learn the pacing of guards. It would swear under oath that I was always moving, never still long enough to murder anyone. At the far end, the only soul awake at 12 a.m. was Murugan, the night watchman. He sat in a plastic chair guarding the service lift, halfdozing in the glow of an IPL replay. I gave him the gentle nod of a sleepless wife fetching chamomile. He answered with a yawn and the universal gesture for *chai*.

Perfect, I thought. *Witnesses who blink too slowly remember even slower.*

*

Raghav was exactly where I'd left him after dinner, propped in the claw-foot tub like a tired deity awaiting worship. The zolpidem from his whisky still fogged his synapses, but he hadn't punched the final clock. His eyes fluttered each time Coltrane's saxophone reached a high note, as though dream and waking life were sharing a fragile lung.

I refreshed the playlist to Mingus' *Goodbye Pork Pie Hat* on a clandestine loop. Jazz that sounds like someone walking themselves to the gallows, step by silksqueaking step.

Steam curled from the water in shy wisps, lukewarm now, deliberately. Warm water accelerates toxins; cold water makes corpses look startled. Lukewarm simply hushes metabolism, the diplomatic temperature of death.

I knelt by the tub, the way a penitent wife might, pulled the vial out and uncapped it. Brotx91 is colourless, odourless, merciless. Seven drops disappear into a bath faster than infidelity under public relations. The surface barely quivered. Even water keeps secrets when you ask politely.

"Sleep?" I whispered.

"Mmm," he croaked, soft as moth wings.

I smoothed his damp hair, an intimacy that felt archival. Then I kissed his forehead. Not for him, but for me. Authors sign their work.

*

There is a noise a body makes when it realises the warranty has expired: not a gasp, not a shout, more a *glitch*. Like an old harddrive hiccupping through corrupted sectors.

Raghav's glitch began at 12:28 a.m. His left hand twitched once, twice, then fell still. Right foot jerked, sending a ripple that nudged the whisky glass against porcelain: *clink*. His breath shortened, clipped into halfsentences. His head lolled forward until his chin met his sternum. The sax solo crested. My pulse did not.

Some reviewers will call this heartless, I thought, *but efficiency is simply compassion without the vanity.*

I reached over and pressed the record button on my phone. The camera faced me, not him, an uninterrupted take of shock forming in real time: eyes widening, lips parting, voice cracking into his name.

Proof that grief was there first.

*

I opened Raghav's MacBook. The draft suicide note glowed, cursor blinking like a mourner unsure where to bow. A few keystrokes adjusted the timestamp to 12:47 a.m.—a time that placed despair before toxin.

"I'm sorry. I tried. But some wounds don't make noise; they just echo."

Echo.

A beautiful word for emptiness. They'll quote that. TV anchors. Psychologists. Poets on Instagram. *An icon of masculinity undone by silence. The last blog of a broken man. We need to talk about men's mental health.*

What none of them would talk about was me. Because I was invisible by design. The wife who looked too composed to be innocent, but too poised to be guilty.

Next, I emptied two blister packs of ZSleep Forte into the bathroom trash, foil packets glinting like modern art. One pack bore his fingerprints, lifted earlier from his whisky glass and dabbed on with forensic finesse. The other, mine, was wiped clean.

I unscrewed the Lagavulin bottle cap, tipped it just enough to mark the 200 ml down; not so much that he'd seem reckless, just resigned.

Finally, I spilt a single teardrop on the keys. Real salt. Authentic. No glycerine. Even monsters have tear ducts.

*

I sat across from him, pretending to scroll through my phone while his breathing slowed. I took his glass when his hand loosened, placed it quietly in the sink. I stayed when his eyelids fluttered and his head dipped lower into the steam curling from the bath.

Brotx91 shuts down the medulla in ninety-eight seconds if administered intravenously; in bathtemperature dermal absorption, it takes six minutes and twenty-one seconds. I counted silently:

0:00: drops vanish

12:28: first twitch

12:54: exhalation stalls

1:41: obituary begins

And then—nothing. No spasm. No last-minute confession. Just the gentle slump of a headline collapsing into lowercase. My watch ticked through each minute. Ten minutes. Fifteen. Twenty.

The sound of water changed, that subtle shift when the body beneath it stops adjusting, stops living. I didn't breathe until I'd checked the pulse myself. Twice.

I dried my hands on a towel, careful to smudge only what needed smudging.

*

5:43 a.m.

When the water cooled to the temperature of the tile, I called the maid. Not too soon— urgency would raise suspicion. Not too late—rot invites questions. Let her phone buzz twice, and cancelled. She would wake, see my missed call, and panicdial back.

She did. "Madam? *Sab theek*—" she began, voice already trembling.

"Leela…" My breath hitched, trembling. "Come… bathroom… Raghav—he's—he's not—" I ended the call mid-sentence. Silence is a better scream.

In less than 20 minutes, the service lift rattled up. The corridor sensors flickered; Murugan followed, curiosity outweighing protocol. The LED haloed around them like stage lighting. I opened the door, robe cinched, mascara smudged artistically by thumb. I let them rush ahead; witnesses prefer initiative.

Leela's shriek ricocheted down twelve floors; Mrs. D'Souza's WhatsApp already buzzed by the second echo.

"Madam, phone ambulance!" Leela cried, panic clawing her voice.

"I—I can't find the number—" I stammered, though I could've recited it backwards in my sleep.

Murugan whipped out his phone, calling it in with just enough tremble in his voice to sound noble.

*

7:17 a.m.

Blue lights strobed the windows; copper and tungsten collided across bathroom tiles. Sub-Inspector Kanade stepped in, shoes politely capped, notebook ready to choreograph the tragedy.

"You found him like this, ma'am?" he asked, flipping the cover with a quiet flourish.

"He wanted a late soak," I murmured. "I fell asleep on the couch." I let my eyelids flutter. Let my voice fracture.

"Any medications?"

I gestured at the half-empty blister packs near the sink. "Sleeping pills. He was… spiralling."

I watched Kanade catalogue the room: neat whisky, half-burned jasmine candle, suicide note blinking on screen. Nothing jarred. Nothing screamed *homicide.*

Dr. Rai tried CPR even though lividity was already quilting the skin. Medics humoured her for protocol. Time of death: 1:45 a.m., they agreed. They were four minutes late, but who counts halfbeats?

*

By 7:45 a.m., the stretcher nudged past the elevator threshold. Heads bowed; some in piety, most in gossip. Phone cameras glowed like votive candles.

I stood at the doorframe, blanketed in Murugan's khaki jacket, hair undone to look undone. One perfect tear traced the path of highlighter down my cheek. Dr. Rai squeezed my shoulder. Diagnosis: admirable composure.

Yes, doctor, I thought, *I practised.*

As the doors hissed shut around Raghav's last ride, Coltrane's sax caught its final breath, held it… Then fell quiet. I let my chest expand. It wasn't grief. It was the certainty that this time, there would be no coming back.

*

Inside the privacy of my skull, a single line typed itself, ready for some distant memoir: *He died peacefully.* Peace is simply the moment after your enemy stops making noise.

I poured myself water. Exactly one sip. Thirst, like grief, must appear real but restrained.

Outside, Mumbai began its morning fidget: milk vans, sky ripening from asphalt to gunmetal blue. The day would call me a *widow*. The news would call him an *icon turned cautionary tale*. The police would call it *case closed*.

And I? I called it *editing*.

"Draft finalised," I whispered to no one.

***

PART *Three*

THE PUBLIC PERFORMANCE

CHAPTER 15:
The Scene of Grief

"Mourning is the last magic trick: the audience knows the dove is hidden, but they still gasp when it flies."

The ambulance shrank down the service road like a bloodred comma, leaving the sentence of our apartment complex unfinished. Once its wail dissolved into the earlymorning smog, the building's façade reverted to concrete indifference: tubes of fluorescent light buzzing overhead, palms trembling in monsoon wind, everything pretending normalcy.

Inside the flat, steam still clung to bathroom tiles, forming ghostglyphs on the mirror. I traced one letter—R—until condensation erased it for me. Housekeeping by humidity. The bathwater, halfdrained, gurgled like a drunk in confession. I pulled the plug, watched the swirl. That's what Raghav had become: a circle finding its own centre before vanishing.

Outside, neighbours gathered. Some for support and others to watch the show. Mr. Anand from 2C, with toothpaste on his chin and guilt in his eyes for enjoying the spectacle. Priya from 3B, barefoot, shawl clutched like a child with a secret. Mrs. Kapoor, third-floor widow, carried the practised tragedy of someone who had survived her own grief but wore it now like an accessory. And the little girl from 5A, thumb in her mouth, eyes wide with the kind of honesty adults don't remember how to hold anymore.

Mrs. Kapoor reached me first. Soft palms, cold rings, perfume mixed with medicated balm. "Aarti *beta*—oh… oh, god… what happened?"

I blinked twice. Not for drama. For rhythm. The first blink was for orientation. The second was for collapse. I folded into her shoulder gently, like someone receiving the word *widow* as a diagnosis, not an identity. She whispered against my ear, "You're ice cold."

She meant my skin. But she didn't know she was naming something truer.

Mr. Anand stepped forward, peeking around the doorframe. "He's been off lately," he muttered. "Poor guy… he's been acting odd lately. Didn't even nod last time I saw him."

The room accepted that comment the way cities accept rain: inevitably, inconvenient, familiar. I didn't speak. I wept harder. Just one silent sob, mouth open, like the echo of someone who forgot how to pray.

*

Inside, Kanade returned with a clipboard and the weariness of a man who had already decided on his conclusion.

"Preliminary report will mention probable self-harm," he said, pen hovering. "No signs of forced entry."

My lips trembled enough to look fragile, not enough to break.

Kanade stepped closer, holding out a clipboard. "Need your signature, ma'am, and the preliminary report."

I took the pen with a slight tremble. "Of course," I said softly, my tone submissive, threaded with just the right note of helplessness.

Cause of incident (prelim): *Suspected self-harm.*

Spouse's demeanour: *Cooperative.*

Remarks: *No signs of forced entry. Lavender candle lit.*

Lavender, I thought, *the colour of half-truths.*

I signed the bottom with a pen that dried up mid-surname. *Poetic,* really—grief misfires halfway through identity.

He folded his notepad. Wiped his face once, like responsibility had made him sweat.

Somewhere behind me, someone filmed. Of course they did. Probably the boy from 2B, the one who once asked Raghav to tag him in a reel. Maybe the maid. Maybe both.

*

Powai General's mortuary wing was painted the colour of clotting milk. I followed the gurney down a corridor lined with plastic flowers, the petals frozen mid-bloom. The airconditioner blasted penitential cold; even my bones apologised.

Dr. Mahika Rai, pathology, greeted me in slippers and a look that blended exhaustion with voyeuristic curiosity. She spoke politely, as if my husband's corpse were a museum piece she'd been asked to dust.

Dr. Rai told me, "We'll need consent for a full post-mortem."

"Of course," I said, making my voice brittle, like cracked porcelain.

"Standard toxicology. Takes seventy-two hours," she informed me.

"Take what you need. He always believed in transparency," I murmured.

The lie tasted metallic. Transparency was Raghav's brand, never his biology.

She offered a plastic chair; I chose to stand. Sitting invites collapse.

*

The mortuary lounge housed three vending machines humming a dirge. A single-use paper cup jittered out, half-filled with sweetened sludge. I cradled it like contraband warmth, then let it cool—sorrow does not swallow comforts too quickly.

Across from me, a young intern, Kabir, tag still creased, scrolled headlines about Raghav's death. The phone's glow painted pity on his cheeks.

"Huge loss, ma'am," Kabir said softly.

I smiled like a scar. "Sanity is a fragile investment."

He blinked, unsure if that was gratitude or a warning.

*

Phone on silent, I watched the screen flicker with pushnotifications; hashtags multiplying like mould on damp bread: #LaughterGoneLoud, #BrokenBlogger, #WidowInWhite.

The real battle wasn't in morgues or police stations; it was on camera lenses and trending pages.

My sobs appeared on neighbourhood WhatsApp groups within the hour. By noon, the first headlines arrived: "*Gone Too Soon: Popular Blogger Found Dead in his Apartment.*"

They called it suicide. They called it a tragedy. They called me "stoic widow." Nobody called it murder.

Brands long ignored my inbox; suddenly, they courted it. A meditation app offered a year-long sponsorship: *"Heal publicly, earn privately."* An NGO pitched a mentalhealth campaign in his name. Opportunism smells like antiseptic: sharp, clean, incapable of rotting itself.

I drafted a single message to Raghav's agent, Sahil: *"Hold all statements. Silence markets better than confusion."*

Then switched the phone off. Dead things deserve company.

*

Through a small rectangular window, I watched Dr. Rai lift Raghav's arm, measure lividity, and log time markers. Her gloved hands moved like calligraphers sketching an obituary only she could read.

The scalpel broke skin at 10:44 a.m. I felt nothing: no quake, no triumph. Just a cool inflation of space behind my ribs, as if someone had opened a secret window to evening air.

He is lighter now, I told myself. *No longer carrying the weight of his own myth.*

*

On my way to file the consent forms, I passed a queue of overnight casualties: a cyclist with bonewhite gauze blooming from his thigh; an old woman clutching an oxygen cylinder like borrowed time. Their eyes followed me, mapping my posture for data on how grief should fit the human frame.

I gave them what they needed: shoulders sloped, steps measured, pupils shining like coins held too long in a closed fist. Empathy is a currency; spend it slowly, or creditors arrive.

*

The hospital elevator smelled of bleach and trepidation. Inside waited Commissioner Vijay Khemka, grey suit rumpled, a man who measured tragedies by column inches. He recognised me by a viral thumbnail alone.

"Mrs. Sharma, condolences. If you need anything, from security to crowd control, call my office," he said.

I tilted my head. "Crowds are flowers, Commissioner. They wilt without sunlight."

Khemka was unsure whether he'd been thanked or dismissed. "...Right."

Doors parted. He left smelling of unresolved guilt. I remained, counted six heartbeats, then pressed *B2*: the morgue again. One must loop back to scenes of crime; repetition irons alibis.

*

Back inside, Dr. Rai had zipped the bodybag. Tag: *SHA-RA-006*. Such bureaucratic neatness. She approached, clipboard in hand. "No external trauma. Toxicology pending, but visual suggests overdose."

I nodded. "He despised needles; pills made more sense."

"Grievances swallow quietly," she said gently.

I almost applauded her poetry.

I placed a palm on the sealed bag, a barrier of vinyl, a promise of crematory fire. Inside, his face was fixed in a neutrality he never managed alive. Fame had fled the musculature.

"Rest now," I whispered, "the headline served its purpose."

*

11:49 a.m.

The taxi dropped me back onto the lobby marble. Night watchman Murugan lowered his cricket radio, eyes shy."Ambulance people said he was peaceful."

"Peace is relative, Murugan. Ask the war what it thinks of the ceasefire."

His confusion tasted like *chai*. I kept walking.

Inside the flat, dawn peeled open the curtains. Light landed on the empty bathtub, milky and innocent. I studied its porcelain gleam: no stain, no whisper. If tubs could testify, they'd still end sentences with question marks.

I shut the door, let the lock click; a period.

*

By noon, a twenty-seven-second video was circulating on every major WhatsApp group in Mumbai. The frozen frame: me, back arched against the doorframe, hand over mouth, mascara trailing downward in soft streaks. Captioned *"Grief in Real Time: Blogger's Widow Breaks Down."* By evening, the hashtags started breeding like algae: #HeartbreakHouse, #MentalHealthMatters, #MasculinityUndone.

The comments: "So young. So tragic," "She looks like she hasn't slept in years," "Was this the cost of comedy?", "Mental health matters. Men matter too."

I didn't reply. I just posted a black square on my Instagram. Caption: "Sometimes silence is the loudest scream. RIP, Raghav." 132k likes. My highest ever.

*

Later that evening, Leela returned to collect her things. Her steps were soft, eyes darting like a girl caught between duty and dread. She paused by the bathroom, looked at the diffuser, then back at me.

"Madam… was this lavender thing on yesterday?" she asked, voice trembling like a loose clothesline in monsoon wind.

I smiled. Gently. Sweetly. "Yes, I lit it after dinner. Why?"

She didn't answer. Just nodded. Something in her eyes, sharp but unspoken. The kind of suspicion that's too young to articulate itself, but too old to forget.

But her eyes darted back to the bathroom once. Then at me. Then away. On the way out, she nearly bumped into the little girl from 5A. Her hand in her nanny's, thumb no longer in her mouth. Just staring at me.

"She insisted on giving you this," the nanny said, embarassed.

The child extended a folded paper crane, wings trembling. "Mama says cranes grant wishes. I wished you wouldn't be lonely."

One beat of humanity. Unexpected. Disarming.

I crouched, accepted the origami. "What colour is the wish?" I asked softly.

"Invisible," the child replied.

I felt a hairline crack in my composure, barely audible, like ice in distant hills. I repaired it with a smile.

"Thank you. Invisible things are the hardest to break."

She nodded, conviction stern, then left. The corridor swallowed her like a secret. I unfolded the crane in the privacy of the closed door. Inside, scrawled in clumsy pencil: *"I saw you smile."*

My heart stuttered.

A cold sweat prickled at the back of my neck. I froze, crane in hand, breath caught in the hollow between rib and reason. I retraced every step from earlier—had I looked too relieved? Had the corner of my mouth twitched at the wrong moment? Had the child seen me *after* the sirens came, or *before*?

Children weaponise honesty without understanding calibre. I burned the note in the sink, ash swirling like furtive snow. Some truths must die younger than their tellers. When I opened the door again, my eyes scanned the corridor—not for adults, not for authorities. For her.

The little girl.

She sat on the stairwell landing, legs swinging, watching the hallway with unnerving stillness. As if waiting for the next scene.

From that moment, I kept her in my periphery. Not obviously. Not foolishly. Just close enough to know where the next truth-bomb might come from.

Because children don't lie. But they don't keep secrets either.

*

The sky bruised into sunrise. I moved through the flat collecting remnants: winestained napkin, a lone cufflink, the half-empty pill blister that would vanquish itself in tomorrow's municipal fire.

I opened the laptop and wrote a single line for the statement Sahil had begged for: *"He made the world laugh; now let the world learn to listen."* I saved it in drafts. The send key can wait. Timing is choreography.

That night, the bed was too wide. The silence stretched, luxurious. No snoring, no ego filling the walls, just air: clean, weightless. I curled into my side of the bed, watching the dent on his side rise back to smoothness, memory uncreasing itself.

"They think the performance ended with applause," I murmured to the dark, "but the encore is just silence wearing darker shoes."

I closed my eyes, and for the first time in two years, the room did not echo his breathing. Only mine, steady and solitary, a metronome rehearsing the next act.

***

CHAPTER 16:

The Grief Blog Begins: Why Women Snap

"If you whisper truth long enough, it turns into liturgy. Scream it, and they dock you for noise pollution."

By sunrise, my apartment was no longer mine. It had become a spectator gallery.

The walls, freshly painted six months ago in muted beige, felt porous, like they had absorbed every WhatsApp forward, every headline, every accusatory blink of a neighbour's eye. The air was thick with lavender, not from grief, but from staging. Grief was a performance now. My grief was *currency.*

At 8:22 AM, the doorbell rang again. Not the police. Not condolence visitors. A journalist.

Not a low-rung intern either, but Payal Kohli. *The* Payal Kohli: prime-time, TRP darling, professional hunter of sobbing women with perfect cheekbones. Her face was already camera-ready, but her voice was cold and off-record.

"Aarti," she purred without asking entry, "I'm not here for an exclusive… I'm here to see." Her smile was feral. "Funny how grief settles so… cleanly on you."

I didn't blink. "Grief is private."

"Private doesn't trend this fast," she snapped back.

She circled my living room, eyes cataloguing the surgical absence of clutter, the staged nostalgia: jasmine incense, Raghav's old guitar perched against a corner, two untouched mugs by the windowsill.

"Too tidy," she said, softer now. "Like you expected to be seen."

I let the silence swell between us, knowing silence was the sharpest confession. She left without drinking the tea I didn't offer.

*

The apartment had settled into a hush so absolute it sounded curated, like the pause a maestro holds before the final crash of cymbals. I lay on Raghav's side of the bed, counting ceilingfan rotations, forty-three per minute, the cadence of a cautious heart. The sheets still carried his ghostly topnote of sandalwood; grief, apparently, is a base note that never quite dries.

Lucidity coiled in my mind like a well-fed serpent: restless, glossy, alert. Grief… didn't feel like grief. It felt like bookkeeping.

I wasn't restless because of what I had done. I wasn't awake because of what I had lost. I was awake because grief was supposed to be consuming, messy, and unstable, and I was too lucid. Too sharp. Too whole. And I knew that would terrify people more than any murder.

I decided grief was being oversold by poets; the real sensation was *surplus wattage.* I rose at 2 a.m., not haunted, but *charged.* Moonlight smuggled itself through halfdrawn blinds, striping the parquet like barcodes. I padded barefoot to the study, the click of the lamp switch sounding like a starting pistol.

*

Raghav's desktop wallpaper, still the two of us in happier sepia, blinked awake. I opened a seldom visited browser profile named *TheOtherHalf*. In college, it had been my sandbox for feminist snark. Tonight, it would be my crucible.

No profile picture. No bio. Just a banner, the colour of latestage bruises and a serif tagline: *"When society asks why we stayed, it forgets who built the cage."*

I flexed my fingers. Control is not a feeling; it is muscle memory. After a homicide, you don't rest; you *cooldown and stretch.*

*

I titled the post *Why Women Snap*. The cursor blinked with judicial impatience. I wrote in crossexamination rhythm, each paragraph an exhibit, every semicolon a breadcrumb: Case law: the frequency of "provoked culpable homicide" defences granted to men, Neurology: cortisol saturation after chronic microhumiliations and Sociology: the algorithm of dismissal—*Hysterical, Unreasonable, Unfeminine*—applied whenever women raise volume above ambient.

Tone? Clinical. The deadliest reports are the quiet ones.

"*Stability is not the absence of wounds; it is the architecture that keeps them hidden until the scaffolding collapses.*"

I avoided anger; anger is a costume they can strip off you. I wore precision, tailored, bulletproof, impossible to misquote.

"Men push. Society watches. Women snap. And then they ask why we didn't leave. Maybe we stopped needing permission."

It wasn't angry. Anger is too cheap, too easy to dismiss. This was academic. Structured. Not a scream, but an affidavit. I wasn't hiding. I was daring them to recognise me by the shape of my restraint.

Paragraph by paragraph, I drafted like I were closing an argument in court. I wasn't explaining rage. I was cross-examining expectation. I didn't say I was justified. I just made sure anyone who read it couldn't fully say I wasn't.

At 1:15 a.m., I pressed *Publish.* The page refreshed, still and unassuming, an unpulled pin waiting for a fingertip.

*

The city outside remained oblivious; taxis idling, stray dogs litigating turf, sodium lamps painting everything antique gold. Yet pixels travel faster than sunrise. At 3:17 am, there were thirty-two shares, at 3:44 am, there were 409 shares, and at 4:10 am, it was 8,000 and counting.

Women trafficked it like contraband medicine: DM, silent group chat, the screenshot courier to sisters sleeping in guest rooms of homes they used to own. I imagined each phone screen lighting up dark kitchens, illuminating bruises that would never post selfies.

*

At 5:00 a.m., I brewed Darjeeling tea with no milk and no sugar. Bitter leaves: Raghav once said they tasted like "women who don't say sorry first." Appropriate.

Steam fogged the kitchen window, and in that temporary mirror, I watched myself swallow. The reflection felt foreign; too awake, too intact. The world expects the newly bereaved to resemble gutted houses; I looked like a locked vault.

"I'm not grieving a man," I told the steam. "I'm grieving the syllabus of obedience he taught me to recite."

*

At 11:02 a.m., I got the first message from a therapist.

"This post sounds like half my client sessions in paragraph form."

I didn't smile for the public. I smiled for myself. Not because I had fooled them, but because they finally sounded like they were catching up to where I'd been sitting for years.

People always think women who snap are unstable. What they never ask is, what happens when an unstable environment meets a stable mind that has simply decided to stop translating itself politely?

I closed my eyes, let the validation skim my pulse like a pebble across water; ripples, not waves. Satisfaction is to revenge what firstaid is to surgery: a preliminary dressing.

*

At noon, my phone rang. It was Sahil, Raghav's agent.

"Aarti… some brands want you for a grief campaign… and, um, just—some people think your composure… It's unnerving."

I let the silence hang. Unnerving. Good.

*

By 2:00 p.m., #WhyWomenSnap trended fourth nationwide, nudged between a cricket scandal and monsoon flood alerts. Influencerpoets converted my lines into pastel infographics; corporate accounts copy-pasted empathy beneath logos.

Trolls arrived on schedule: @AlphaRealist: "Another widow monetising trauma," @TradBro420: "If men wrote this, it'd be called hate speech," @SadhuInSneakers: "Touch grass, lady."

I archived every slur into a folder titled *Exhibits: Misogyny, 4th Ed.* Not for litigation, but for pattern study. Patterns make predictions; predictions keep you ten moves ahead.

*

Later that afternoon, Payal returned. Camera-ready again, but this time live, mic clipped to her collar. Off-camera, she whispered, "You scare people, Aarti. You don't *look* like a victim."

The red light blinked on. "Tell us," Payal asked, the voice pitched just right for mass consumption, "How do you find strength after such personal loss?"

I smiled. Slow. Controlled. "I don't 'find' strength, Payal. I manufacture it."

*

The clip went viral within two hours. "*Grief Manufacturing—the Widow Who Won't Cry*."

Hate piled in faster than sympathy. Anonymous accounts dissected my body language frame by frame. Conspiracy theories sprouted: Was I too calm? Too articulate? Too coordinated?

Exactly what I wanted. When people debate *how* you grieve, they stop looking at *why* you grieve.

*

That night, I reviewed the footage of myself on loop. Paused. Rewinded. Zoomed in on my own face. Noted the microexpressions. Adjusted eye moistness by 10%. Angled shoulders for greater frailty. Kept the lip quiver subtle, not performative.

Tomorrow's performance would be better. I drafted the second post: *She Stayed Too Calm, So They Never Heard the Thunder*. Seven-minute read. Goes live tonight at 9:45 p.m., the hour when domestic lights dim and browser histories grow honest. That's when women are quietest in public but loudest in their minds. After the dishes. After putting the children to bed. After texts from bored men who call them complicated after forgetting their birthdays. Right when the world stopped needing them and their own thoughts became unbearable.

Between paragraphs, I built loaded silences, the kind that make readers inhale as though oxygen costs extra.

*

By the next morning, it was a graphic. Then a meme. Then a screensaver. Then a threat. What they didn't know was that I didn't want to be a movement. I didn't want followers. They said I gave them language, but I didn't.

I gave them a mirror without distortion. I wanted women to have mirrors. Untouched by filters. Mirrors that didn't make you beautiful, just accurate. And women finally saw themselves not as hysterical, but cornered.

Women reposted it while ignoring apology texts that began with "You're too sensitive."

They reposted it while stirring tea alone in kitchens that once smelled like Sunday family lunches. They reposted it with bruises still forming under sleeves, or with court documents unopened, or with unopened emails from HR marked *Personal.*

It wasn't activism. It was architecture. I wasn't just grieving. I was grieving on behalf of a gender. And that kind of grief? It scales.

I was grieving the architecture of expectations I'd been raised inside, brick by brick, like a daughter learning which parts of herself made people uncomfortable and which parts made her employable.

I never claimed authorship. Not in the comments. Not in the shadows. I didn't need to. Truth leaves its own watermark in punctuation and pain.

By midnight, suspicion started to grow. People wondered aloud on message boards. A viral tweet speculated: *"The widow writes like a surgeon who learned that scalpels cut chains, too."*

I screenshotted it. Good literature deserves a footnote.

*

Midafternoon: the apartment was silent but for the rhythmic tick of the wall clock, a metronome for strategic grief. I opened the balcony doors; Mumbai's humidity coiled around my ankles like ankleweights, grounding, reminding. Below, schoolgirls giggled at something on a phone, maybe my post, maybe cat videos. Both can catalyse revolution under the right hormones.

I leaned on the rail, spoke to the vacancy where Raghav's voice once lived: "You asked why women talk in riddles. Because straight truths get us labelled difficult. So, we built labyrinths you never learned to navigate."

Wind swallowed the confession and went on rustling laundry lines.

*

Twilight bled into the livingroom corners. I proofread the scheduled post; fingers steady as a sniper's: "A stable mind, when surrounded by unstable expectations, is mistaken for madness once it decides to stop translating itself politely."

Satisfied, I shut the lid. A low hum of far-off traffic echoed like applause. I steeped another cup of uncompromising tea and watched the sodium lamps ignite one by one, each a lighthouse for nocturnal conspiracies.

Somewhere inside those amber circles, new readers waited, women on balconies, men in denial, detectives drawing lines on bulletin boards. They would meet my words in twenty-one thousand seconds.

And me? I would be right here, eyes sharp, heart untroubled, listening to the collective click of mirrors turning toward harsh light.

***

CHAPTER 17: #BelieveWidows vs. #JusticeForRaghav

"You know you've won when your silence speaks louder than their hashtags."

They say silence is safety. They've never met a woman who knows silence is a signature.

It started where everything always starts now, with an airless Reddit thread buried four tabs deep in a stranger's browser, typed out under the flicker of a second-hand ceiling fan, somewhere between loneliness and caffeine.

r/TrueCrimeIndia. Not big. Not polished. Just humid with suspicion. Mostly men. Mostly profiles with names like *FactFinder87* and *IndJusticeWarrior.* Mostly the kind of users who thought their Wi-Fi connection qualified them as detectives, jury, and God.

The title of the thread was low-budget thriller material: "*Something Doesn't Add Up About Raghav Kapoor's Suicide.*" No evidence. Just tone.

Underneath, there were screenshots. Pixelated. Zoomed and cropped by fingers that still smelled of potato chips. Me, outside the crematorium, hands folded, not *clasped*, folded. My eyes were on the priest, not downcast like they wanted. My *saree*: pale blue. Not widow-white. And their caption, written in that particular font of digital male outrage: "*This isn't mourning. This is marketing.*"

I didn't react. I just watched it unfold like I'd watch an overcooked *paratha* flake apart: inevitable, messy, but ultimately forgettable.

Then the comments multiplied, like cockroaches in a rental flat no one wanted to claim responsibility for. "*She wore blue. That's not grief. That's branding.*" "*Look at her face. Calm as an accountant filing someone else's taxes.*" "*She's emotionally regulated like a defence attorney giving her own eulogy.*"

And then, under that, one lone reply: "*She* is *a lawyer, dude.*"

For a moment, I felt almost grateful for that stranger. Almost.

But then came the escalation, the ones who didn't need logic, just a scent of disorder to chew on. "*Slow homicide. Emotional dehydration. A woman like that doesn't kill fast,*" "*She's an Indian Amy Dunne. Just less contouring,*" "*She probably logged his symptoms like monthly bills.*"

They thought they were inventing a conspiracy. All they were doing was finally catching up to me.

But the one that stopped me cold, the one I screenshotted and stored, not for evidence, but for symmetry, was posted by someone anonymous, no photo, no bio, just the user handle: *BelieverInPatterns.*

Top upvoted comment: "*You don't hate her because she might be guilty. You hate her because she didn't cry when you wanted her to.*"

Pinned by democracy.

*

Outside of Reddit, the battle unfolded like a badly staged opera. #BelieveWidows. #JusticeForRaghav. Two hashtags. Two sides. Neither of them were mine. I hadn't picked this war. But then again, when you inherit the ruins of a man's reputation, you don't get to choose whether people worship the ashes or demand an autopsy.

Feminist accounts called me resilient. Podcasts quoted me like I was both an elegy and a prophet. Instagram stories paired my Foundation speech with pastel filters and cursive captions: "*She didn't cry because she already knew how to rebuild.*"

Meanwhile, the men's rights podcasts woke up from their afternoon naps to call me *dangerous*. One anchor on a regional channel tilted his head into the camera and said the phrase I could've scripted myself: "*Is this India's* Gone Girl *moment?*"

I didn't respond. I didn't need to. The machinery was already running on its own battery, charged by centuries of discomfort with women who knew how to narrate their own grief without asking for proofreading.

*

In the middle of it all, publishers arrived like realtors at a murder scene: "*We'd love to amplify your story.*" They pitched titles like gravestones. "*Widowed and Rising,*" "*Her Grief, His Silence,*" "*After the Bath.*"

One particularly eager editor sent me a line that I printed out and folded neatly into the spine of my journal: "Think *Gone Girl* meets *Michelle Obama.*"

They didn't want my story. They wanted the shape of it. They wanted to be next to the explosion without paying for the shrapnel.

I didn't reply. I created a folder called: "*When They Want My Voice.*" Inside it, a subfolder: "*Leverage.*" Not a memoir. Ammunition.

And the hashtags kept multiplying like mould, like damp stains in old Mumbai buildings that no one wants to admit are terminal.

*

At mid-morning, the doorbell rang. The little girl from 5A appeared, clutching a notebook. Her nanny hovered, embarrassed.

"Aunty, my teacher said draw what bravery looks like," the girl said. She opened the notebook: a stick figure in a blue *saree*, mouth a straight line, eyes wide open. "Is this right?"

I nodded; my throat lined with ash. She left. Nanny mouthed *sorry for bother*. I closed the door and felt the faultline widen: children see a silhouette, adults demand an autopsy.

*

That evening, I abandoned the apartment for the airport lounge. It was neutral ground, anonymity polished by duty-free cologne. As I glided through security, eyes followed: sympathy, suspicion, desire to witness a viral widow in unfiltered motion.

A woman touched my wrist gently. Mid-thirties. Expensive watch. Perfect nails. She leaned in as if we were cousins from some parallel life.

"I'm sorry for your loss," she whispered. "You're not like other widows."

I wanted to say, *other widows bury husbands. I buried a storyline.* But I smiled. Small. Composed. The kind of smile you give when you don't have time to translate your real answer into something polite enough for strangers.

A few feet away, a young journalist watched me too long while pretending to scroll through his phone. I knew what he wanted. A photo, maybe. A headline. Maybe both.

*

Hotel room. 1:03 a.m.

The city lights patterned the ceiling like data points. I opened *TheOtherHalf* and drafted a new post: *Silence Is a Signature*. Six-minute read. Schematic prose dissecting why society confuses quiet women with forgiven women.

"When a man grieves quietly, we call it stoic. When a woman does, we call it sinister."

Scheduled it for 9:45 p.m., the hour statisticians call Peak Isolation.

*

Laptop closed, I poured whisky—not Lagavulin, a new bottle untouched by memory. I raised the glass to the window where hashtags flicker across billboards.

"My silence," I toasted, "is the earthquake sensor you refuse to read."

Sip. Bitter. Perfect.

*

Before I slept, I stood before the mirror, shoulders squared, posture controlled. No mascara tonight. No illusion. Just me, face bare, pulse steady.

The media had tried to disarm me with sentiment. The trolls tried to drown me in suspicion. But I wasn't built to survive. I was built to outlast.

*

The last line I whispered to my reflection, sharp enough to cut through static: "Innocent women cry to be believed. Clever women don't need belief. They just need enough silence to win."

And silence… was my native tongue.

*

I reclined on the starched hotel sheets, phone buzzing with the roar of strangers adjudicating my morality. Let them. In every notification, I heard the creak of narrative moving its own furniture, exactly as planned.

Because they would never find a confession. Only structure. And structure is harder to disprove than motive. Because in a world that punishes loud women and doubts quiet ones, silence isn't safety, it's strategy.

And I was fluent. Not in innocence. Not even in rage. In composition. Clean. Coiled. Quiet. Just like a signature you don't need to spell it anymore because by now, everyone knows it's yours.Top of Form

Eyes drifted shut. Sleep finally came, quiet, clinical, unrepentant.

"The war is no longer about innocence," I reminded the dark, "it's about punctuation. And I had already placed the full stop."

***

CHAPTER 18: Foundation of Sympathy

"They say grief humbles you. I say it franchises you."

The clicks began before I stepped out of the black sedan.

Cameras perched on shoulders, eyes hidden behind sunglasses, microphones lurching forward like impatient questions. The venue wasn't a memorial—it was a stage with better lighting. A ballroom at one of South Mumbai's most discreet hotels, now brimming with journalists hungry to package sorrow into digestible narratives.

The orchids smelled expensive. Imported, probably. The kind that doesn't belong to this heat, this city, or to grief itself, but money loves irony. White petals curling perfectly around borrowed glass vases, soft light reflecting off the satin ribbons that knotted around the neck of every chair. A stage at the far end, draped in cream, with one enormous vinyl print behind it: "The Raghav Kapoor Foundation for Men's Mental Health."

The irony wasn't just in the flowers. It was in the fact that the logo, all lowercase, tastefully minimalist, had been designed by one of the same digital agencies that used to pitch influencer campaigns to Raghav before his hashtags started sounding tired.

Now he was a hashtag himself. And I was standing in its shadow.

I stood in the waiting lounge, palms steady, pulse quiet. The black *saree* I wore had been selected after two hours of lighting tests; the fabric dulled under daylight but softened beautifully under spotlights. No lipstick. Bare cheeks. *Kajal* just deep enough to make exhaustion look earned. Simple silver studs in the ears, nothing that reflected light. I wanted to look like someone who had stopped wearing jewellery, not because of grief, but because she didn't need accessories anymore. Only conviction.

But beneath the surface, something splintered. The media weren't behaving.

Minutes before the speech, a junior producer cornered me by the glass doors. "Ma'am… word from the desk… Channel Eight's planning to break a segment tonight," he murmured. "They've obtained private CCTV footage. You walking into your building the morning of the… incident."

I blinked once, and that was my only tell.

He continued, "There's a debate trending already. People are saying your composure… looked practised. Too practised."

For the first time, my throat dried.

*

The host's voice summoned me onto stage, smooth and rehearsed: "…widow turned activist… India's brave voice for men's mental health."

Applause rose. Loud. Controlled.

I walked onto the stage at exactly eleven. Not eleven-oh-two. Eleven sharp. That's how you show composure, not by crying, but by being punctual.

The applause wasn't immediate. They were still calibrating the performance. Then the first pair of hands met in the middle of the room. Female. Age fifty-five, probably. Upper arm softened by years of lifting kitchen vessels and lowering expectations. Her claps gave permission to the rest. Warm. Long. The kind of applause you give a woman who has endured something but didn't bleed publicly. They don't trust bleeding. They prefer survivors who come pre-sanitised.

The first line of the speech was rehearsed so perfectly that it didn't sound rehearsed at all. "In grief, we often think we are alone. I am here to make sure no man—no person—ever feels alone again."

Pause. Measured. Eyes lowered. They leaned in.

"In Raghav's memory, I am launching this foundation to ensure that no man ever has to suffer silently again."

The pause was engineered. I studied orators, trial lawyers, and even failed TED Talks. I knew the pause was where the power sat. Silence makes the audience lean forward. It makes them complicit.

Then I bowed my head. Not dramatically. Just enough to signal humility. In that moment, I was not Aarti Kapoor. I was infrastructure. Legacy in human form.

The keynote followed. Dimmed house lights. Gold curtain draped behind me like someone had mistaken mourning for celebration. I stood behind the podium and delivered grief like a verdict.

"Grief is not loud," I said softly. "It's something you learn to fold into your voice."

I heard a woman in the third row sniff. I could smell sandalwood from someone's prayer bead bracelet nearby. I imagined every seat holding a woman who hadn't cried properly in five years, or a man rehearsing bravery so long he forgot the language for helplessness.

"Raghav tried," I said. "He reached out. It just… wasn't enough."

My throat caught on "enough." I made sure of it. I sip water; not for hydration, but for humanity. That's the thing about performing pain—you don't perform the words. You perform the hesitations between them.

I continued: "We tell men to be strong. We never ask if they're tired of being statues."

A man nodded. A teenager wiped his eyes. I let my eyes scan the room without focusing on anyone. That's the trick: look like you're searching for someone you already lost.

*

By the time I returned to my seat, a notification vibrated in my clutch. An anonymous email, with the subject line: "Video circulating. Watch your back." The attachment was a thirty-second clip of me from security footage, collected posture, purposeful steps, and zero falter. The caption said: "Why is she walking like a CEO after a merger, not a widow after a death?"

*

The after-panel interviews were more hostile. More intrusive. Three journalists, one mental health advocate, and a moderator who clearly thought grief makes you soft.

She smiled tightly, then asked: "Aarti, your poise has been… exceptional. But critics say your foundation has shifted focus from Raghav's career to your own narrative. How do you respond to that?"

I paused, tilted my head and let my silence stretch just long enough to feel unscripted. Then, I answered the way trial lawyers answer when they know the jury already loves them. "If telling my story keeps one man from swallowing silence, I'll wear every label they give me."

The room moved with the sound of approval. Collective exhale. Even the moderator smiled, tight at the corners, as if she wanted to resist the warmth but had already lost.

I smiled, then added softly: "Besides… I lost my husband. Surely, I'm allowed to find my voice?"

That line became a headline before the panel ended. I didn't have to convince anyone I was broken. Just that I'd been neatly rearranged.

By evening, social media spiralled. One headline flashed across televisions in the hotel lobby: "*India's Most Composed Widow: Heroine or Manipulator*?" Two weeks later, the circuit began. NDTV. Mint Lounge. A pop-up panel at a Gurgaon WeWork about *burnout among start-up CEOs.* I didn't say no. Not because I wanted their sympathy. Because I wanted their bandwidth.

I was on NDTV: *"The Cost of Masculine Silence"*, I spoke at a tech company: *"High-Performance Men and the Quiet Breakdown"*, I published an op-ed in *The Hindu*: *"His Grief, My Voice"*.

All the people who never once checked if I was happy in the last four years suddenly wanted my thoughts on gender, trauma, and the masculine condition. The media called me: "India's Most Graceful Widow," "The Face of Feminist Grief," and "The Widow Who Speaks for the Silenced."

I was no longer *his* widow. I was *India's* widow. I didn't fight it. Grace wears better than guilt, and it fits interviews like silk draping around my bones, hiding the fact that I once considered screaming the truth in a courtroom.

A woman at one event caught my wrist between her trembling hands.

"You're so strong," she whispered, like she was confessing a sin. "If it were me, *beta*… I'd be in pieces."

I wanted to tell her the truth: I was in pieces. I had just alphabetised them. Instead, I smiled with the softness of a woman who'd practised gentle grief in three different mirrors before sunrise.

One night, after an event, as I stood by the refreshments table, a production assistant approached me, the kind of boy who carried tripods badly but ambition well. His cheeks were pink with too much coffee, too much Twitter, too much wanting to be noticed without quite deserving it.

"Ma'am… your speech was unforgettable."

I nodded politely. Then came the sting.

"You're too composed," he added under his breath, trying to make it sound admiring but failing. "Like… you practised it."

I met his eyes and held them. "I did."

He blinked. The kind of blink that doesn't mean understanding, only disbelief.

"Some women cry," I said softly. "Some rehearse. Some do both."

He didn't know whether to smile or flinch. So, he did neither. He just stepped backwards. I turned, heels soft against the carpet. My footsteps sounded like punctuation.

Outside, photographers were already waiting, cameras half-lowered like they hadn't decided if I was a story or a shrine. Flash. Flash. Flash. Grief with definition. Widowhood with contouring. I paused just once to let them get the full shape of my posture. And in that space between shutter clicks, the next headline formed itself like a birth: *"India's Grieving Widow Teaches the Nation How to Heal."*

And somewhere inside me, the final line of my next blog post formed: "When they brand you with sympathy, use it to pay for your next stage."

They thought I was building a foundation. But really? I was building permanence. A myth so neatly composed that even I wouldn't be able to fully untangle it later. Not a tombstone. A cathedral.

And when they walked inside it to pray, they'd have no idea that the marble was laid with rage, the ceiling painted with evidence, and the whole altar built on a single, steady hand, mine.

Outside, the world debated whether my grief was real. Inside, I smiled, slightly crooked this time. They wanted cracks in my mask? Let them wonder if it was breaking. It wasn't. It was tightening.

*

Because in a world that photographs every tear, sometimes the cleanest shot is the one where you refuse to fall apart.

And I was just getting started.

In a world obsessed with cracking women open to examine their pain, I gave them a polished surface too smooth to shatter. And beneath that surface, I prepared for the next chapter, one where survival wasn't enough. It had to look like sainthood, while hiding something far colder beneath.

***

CHAPTER 19:

Mira Rao: The Woman Who Didn't Blink

"There are two kinds of women you can't lie to: mothers and former homicide detectives. Only one of them smiles when you make a mistake."

It wasn't the accusation that unsettled me. It was the attention. You don't *meet* a woman like Mira Rao; you inherit her presence like a shadow, without ceremony, without sound. Before I ever heard her voice, I'd heard of her: not in newspapers, not in press clips, but in muttered warnings passed between polished boardrooms and unpolished police stations.

She didn't crash into your life. She entered like an old draft under a closed door—cold, creeping, uninvited.

The venue was one of those washed-out suburban hotel conference rooms, the kind where grief goes to dress up and wear foundation. Grief-themed panels are taxidermy displays, sorrow stuffed, pinned, and arranged under downlights so bystanders can feel cultured for staring. This one squatted in a suburban hotel ballroom the colour of expired milk. Airconditioning gnawed at my joints; orchids shivered in their vases like debutantes regretting the invitation.

The title on the LED backdrop said *Masculinity & Modern Grief*, PR intern feminism, equal parts earnest and anaemic.

Four men bracketed me, sweating under linen blazers but desperate to look compassionate. Tissues lay beside the microphones, white flags waiting for tears on command. I wore the widow's smile version 4.0: seasoned, symmetrical, SPF 50.

That's when I noticed her in the fifth row, dead centre.

Beige *kurta*, hair knotted without vanity, cheap sandals. No phone, no badge. A single fountain pen balanced between fingers, as though ink alone could excavate truth. She did not watch me; she measured me, her eyes steady, unhurried, unblinking. Courtrooms had taught me the chill of being examined as evidence, but Mira Rao's gaze felt colder, architectural: checking load-bearing walls for hidden rot.

I looked away first. A tactical retreat.

*

After the session, she didn't approach me immediately. She waited. By the tea counter, as the last of the reporters scrambled for soundbites, Mira appeared at my shoulder. Quiet. Deliberate.

Her voice slid through my composure. "You misquoted the timeline."

I glanced sideways. "Excuse me?"

"You said you found him at 6:15 a.m. The ambulance was called at 6:08. Curious detail… when the heart stops, memory tends to sharpen, not smudge."

My throat clenched. I smiled mechanically. "Trauma distorts recollection."

"Or clarifies it," she replied softly. "Depends on which side of the timeline you stand on."

She didn't need to raise her voice. She just placed a scalpel on the table and let me decide if I was already cut.

"I'm not here to accuse. Only to observe," she said quietly.

I smiled like I was amused. Like women smile when men tell them to relax. Controlled. Professional. "Most men said that to me, too," I said, reaching for the sugar spoon. "Right before they judged."

She didn't correct me. Didn't defend herself. Just sipped the watery conference tea and nodded, as if I'd just passed some invisible test.

But I knew then: she wasn't here for a headline. She was here for an audit. And audits don't clap. They *calculate.*

*

She didn't need introductions. She was one of those women Mumbai remembers between glass towers, not in page three spreads, but in the spaces between scandals, where retired lawyers pass names like passwords.

"Used to work homicide. Walked away mid-case. too uncooperative for politics and too correct for corruption. The kind who didn't crave the spotlight but knew how to pivot it. Whispers said she didn't solve cases. She dissolved them."

Insomnia later drove my cursor across midnight. *Mira Rao* yielded almost nothing except digital negative space. Scattered breadcrumbs: Ex-IPS. Former Delhi Crime Branch. Dropped out mid-career because, as one forgotten interview said, *"the system got too noisy to hear the quiet truths."* Master's in Psychology. Published once in a journal nobody reads but everyone references when they want to sound credible. Thesis: *The Language of Control in Domestic Violence.*

Another link hooked me. *'Woman IPS officer cracks serial domestic abuse cover-up in Gurgaon, says the killer wasn't a person, it was neglect."* A grainy photo. Mira in uniform. Eyes sharp enough to cut fabrications in half.

The line stayed with me. *'The killer wasn't a person. It was neglect."*

I sat back.

Buried deeper was an old case file from 2014. Victim: Shraddha A., twenty-seven, suicide. Complaint before that: dismissed. Six months between warning and death. Mira's name was signed at the bottom of the file, followed by the transfer notice.

She didn't leave systems. She left the noise. That's what made her dangerous. She wasn't chasing crimes anymore. She was hunting unfinished endings.

I wasn't scared. Not exactly. But something shifted. The sensation of a loose thread somewhere in the lining of a favourite dress. You know it's not going to tear today. But it *knows* you know it's there.

Mira's signature wasn't her writing. It was *what happened to other people after she left.* Not violence. Rearrangement. She didn't catch you in the act. She invited you to narrate your own confession, word by word, until you realised you'd delivered it in neat stanzas, gift-wrapped for your own trial.

The terrifying part wasn't that she suspected me. It was that she wasn't *after* me. Not yet. She was after the *shape* of the thing. The scaffolding. The unspoken logic. Because Mira Rao didn't solve murders anymore. That's why she frightened me: she no longer chased crimes. She audited unfinished stories. And mine was still damp with ink. I was sitting on a first draft with excellent punctuation and just enough wrong tension to smell like preparation.

*

For weeks, I watched for her shadow everywhere. I started to hear her style of thinking in articles that used words like *curated* or *intentional grief*, not written by her, but *influenced.* That's how Mira operated. Not in accusations. In *edits.*

Her reach was ambient. It wasn't that I was afraid of being caught. It was that I was afraid of being *understood*. There's no alibi against being understood.

*

After yet another panel called *Courage in Widowhood*, I rehearsed sincerity in a mirror framed by peeling gold leaf. Her reflection slotted in behind mine, quiet as gravity.

When I turned, she spoke as if we'd always been mid-conversation. "You're very composed," she said. Not warm. Not cruel. Observational.

"It's good training," I answered before I could stop myself.

"Training's for sports," she murmured. "What you have? That's choreography."

And the way she said *choreography* sounded like she was describing something lovely, yet slightly incorrect.

I almost respected her. I almost liked her. What unsettled me wasn't her competence. It was the stillness. Everyone else tried to make me *react*, including reporters, hashtags, and even old friends pretending they wanted comfort.

Mira? Mira didn't *interrupt* me. She waited until I mispronounced myself.

That night, I deleted two scheduled blog posts. Rewrote another three. It wasn't about guilt. It was about *proofreading* my performance.

Mira wasn't hunting mistakes; she was cultivating them.

*

Back in my flat, something was off. Laptop open. Notifications muted. One anonymous message at the top: "Why did your charity bank account open three days before his death?"

A cold sweat prickled on my forehead.

*

The next morning, Mira's number flashed on my phone. Her message was simple: "Lunch. You pick the place. I'll pick the questions."

*

We met at a roadside Irani café. Low ceilings, flickering tube lights, the kind of establishment where big egos shrank. She didn't take out a notebook. She didn't record. She just stirred her chai like a woman willing to stay until I blinked first.

I crossed my legs, smiled, armour polished. She skipped the predictable questions about depression, arguments, and warning signs. Instead, she asked, "Did you ever hate him?"

The room moved differently after that. Not the air. The gravity. I could've lied. Could've gone sentimental. Could've gone poetic. I didn't.

My voice was even. "Hate keeps the dead alive. I prefer efficiency."

She didn't write that down. Not my words. My *cadence*. I could feel her measuring me, not for guilt, but for coherence. She wasn't trying to solve a murder. She was testing an argument.

"Your TED talk," she said. "In the third answer, you claimed you and Raghav reconciled weeks before his death."

I nodded.

"Curious. The final WhatsApp backup from his phone doesn't have a single message to you after the 18th."

I inhaled sharply. Mira didn't miss it. She leaned in, voice so gentle it almost sounded maternal. "You see, Aarti… I don't chase confessions. I build the ecosystem where guilt becomes too heavy to carry quietly."

I stood to leave after the hour. She let me. Didn't follow the usual detective lines. Didn't warn. Didn't hint. Just let the silence do the work of doubt. Right before I touched the door handle, she asked one thing.

"Do you still read his blogs?"

I paused. One breath too long. Then tilted my head like a woman performing resignation. "Closure requires amnesia."

"Amnesia is fragile." She smiled. For the first time. And not kindly.

*

Back home, reflexes disobeyed theory. I opened Raghav's archive, with its Helvetica arrogance, sepia photos. Scrolled to a post from thirty-two days before his bathwater eulogy. Buried comment, unsigned: *"Stories end when the wrong narrator goes silent."*

My pulse misstepped. Was that his? I felt something behind my ribs shift, sharp and sudden, like someone had slipped a blade between muscle and memory. I closed the laptop. Sat perfectly still, like a woman caught rehearsing the wrong scene.

It wasn't fear. Not exactly. It was the terrible, holy realisation.

*

That night, the mirror no longer reflected an unshakable widow. It reflected a woman suddenly aware that the wrong person had been watching her all along. Mira didn't need proof. She needed duration. Duration plus pattern equals confession.

I was no longer writing; I was revising, defensive, breathless, late. Grief used to be my language. Performance, my mask.

But Mira? Mira didn't chase stories. She audited endings. And mine? Mine had just been reopened.

***

CHAPTER 20: Evidence, Alphabetised

"Crimes can be buried. Patterns… they resurrect themselves."

It began with bureaucracy: an email titled "*Asset Valuation Visit: Policy #4711B.*" Corporate politeness translated into extortion: *Open every drawer or forget the ₹35 lakh cheque.*

At 10:46 a.m., the peephole framed a procession: the Claims officer in overstarched linen, hugging clipboards instead of condolences, two constables wearing bodycams and boredom, and Mira Rao masked as a *RiskAssessment Analyst*, but her eyes still carried post-mortem humidity.

They didn't need my permission. They came with paper armour: warrants, inventories, and custody logs. The hinges sighed as the door gave way. My apartment inhaled them like an infection it couldn't resist. And somewhere under the scent of jasmine and sanitiser, I tasted it.

The slow, suffocating arrival of an *audit.*

*

The walkthrough began. My flat, suddenly foreign, was dissected into zones.

Kitchen

Steel ladles freckled with turmeric; a virgin wok glinting with the shame of unused gifts. The constable photographed spice jars as if masala could launder money.

Bedroom

Sarees vacuumpacked into translucent coffins. My widowhood curated; creases sharp, empathy ready for editorial spreads. Mira's fingers brushed the edge of my bedside drawer, hovering over a single unopened book: Raghav's last gift.

"Unseal, document," she said, not looking at me.

I stood by the doorframe. Smiling was no longer useful. Breathing felt optional.

Then came the **Study Room**. My last defence. I watched her pause in the doorway, reading the air. The room smelled of printer ink, dried sandalwood, and something older, something sour. My muscles coiled.

Her fingers skimmed the bookshelf: Kafka to corporate law to *Kama Sutra*, alphabetised, symmetrical, curated like everything else in my life. Then, there was a fractional pause. Between *Men Are from Mars* and *The Art of War*, her gloved fingers slipped through a narrow void. Resistance. She probed, slower this time. Leather whispered against her palm. Black Moleskine. Scarred spine. Pages swollen from humidity and… something else.

"E17," she murmured.

Flash. Seal. Tag.

I tasted metal in my mouth.

On the lower shelf was another glitch. A brittle cash box, yellowing invoices, and a pharmacy blister pack dated within spitting distance of Raghav's last bath.

"E18."

The zipper on the evidence pouch zipped up like a noose tightening. Throughout, Mira spoke only to her clipboard. Silence handled the interrogation. She didn't ask questions. She didn't have to.

*

Late afternoon

The building's community hall with fluorescents hissing, plastic orchids nodding like accomplices. On a folding table, Mira slit the evidence pouch of E17 and opened the journal beneath twin lenses; one departmental, one personal.

Ink scratched with surgical precision: On 14 Feb: *"She touched my wrist the way nurses test pulse, hoping for silence."* On 22 March: *"If I die quietly, ask her why she looks rested."*

The constable shifted awkwardly. Mira didn't flinch. Page 56 coughed up a folded receipt: rice, ginger, clove oil, Diphenhydramine, circled twice. One circle wobbled—Raghav's tremor. The second was prosecution steady—mine.

My heartbeat filed a motion to adjourn.

Mira's voice was nearinaudible. "Dual handwriting. Log it."

No verdict stated. Oxygen, nonetheless, thickened into evidence.

*

Forensic laptop. Writeblocker hummed like a refrigerated drawer. *AltLife_v2.xlsx* autorecovered, cells razed to white. Metadata proved deletion at 12:15 a.m., the night the ashes cooled.

Mira copied the SHAhash, initialled the chainform, and resealed the staticproof pouch. The policy officer sighed, premium protected. Mira's eyes stayed lit, a riddle backlit by certainty.

*

At 4:15 p.m., the circus was packed up, and the evidence chain was sealed. Moleskine bagged. Blister packs tagged. Metadata backed up twice. The official signatures were collected like cold insurance policies.

Before leaving, Mira lingered in the doorway. She pressed the key into my palm, glove brushing metal as if checking for a phantom pulse. No lecture. No accusation. Just one observation.

"Phase one complete," she said softly, pressing the cold house key into my palm.

Her hand paused, a fraction too long, as if feeling for tremor beneath my skin. Our eyes locked. Hers said, "I'm not looking for guilt. I'm mapping structure."

Mine replied: "Chapters still under revision."

But in that brief second, I felt it crack.

She turned; the hallway swallowed her clipboard steps. The furniture remained where she'd found it, yet every object now leaned infinitesimally toward confession, like soldiers awaiting reveille.

I locked the door, listened to the bolt click, and heard, deep in my ribs, a book fall from a shelf that no longer existed. "A secret isn't undone by discovery," I told the dim room, "only by cataloguing."

Mira wasn't guessing anymore. She was alphabetising me, filing me, preparing my narrative for forensic analysis. And in that sterile quiet, I realised the worst truth. I had run out of furniture to rearrange.

And Mira Rao had just started reading.

***

CHAPTER 21:
Conversation in Red ink

"When an editor slides your life back across the table, it is never for proofreading. It is to prove the draft was never yours."

Dead men should stay buried. But Raghav Kapoor had always refused to shut up, even in death.

The whisper arrived not as a phone call or subpoena, but in the form of black leather: thick, matte, blood-warm in touch, stitched down the spine like an old wound refusing to scab over. No name embossed. No title. Just the quiet arrogance of something that had already outlived its author.

The police had missed it, of course. Their eyes were trained for the theatrical: pill bottles, whisky tumblers, the curated wreckage of a man known to blog his breakdowns. But grief doesn't scream. It hides. In margins. In forgotten shelves behind self-help books. In the spaces between performance and pathology.

Mira found it. Of course she did. Not like a detective. Like a woman who's spent a lifetime archiving the damage men leave behind in lowercase fonts. She was careful with it. Almost reverent. Like the journal could still bleed if you opened it wrong.

She didn't call the press. She called me. The message was brief. No official stamp, no summons, no lawyer CC'ed.

Mira Rao: *Tea. My office. One hour.*

The attached photograph was worse than a subpoena. The Moleskine journal: Raghav's. The one I was sure hadn't survived the last cleanup.

*

Her office wasn't sterile like police stations. It was too quiet, too orderly, like it hosted postmortems of stories, not corpses. Two chairs, one teapot, no recorder, no file marked *suspect*, just a soft ceramic clink and a room arranged like a polite ambush.

She handed me the journal like a priest handing over a final confession. I didn't touch it, not immediately. I watched it instead, as if it might open itself, speak aloud, betray me with its spine. Then I picked it up the way one holds a snake: firm, deliberate, knowing it won't bite unless provoked.

No headings. No formatting. Just scattered lines, floating on paper like bruises that never reached the skin. "*She stopped talking three weeks ago,*" "*Today she touched my arm like she was testing the temperature of water,*" "*I'm not sure if she's grieving something that already happened, or something she's planning,*" "*She sleeps folded. Like architecture,*" "*If I die peacefully, check if she's rested the next day.*"

That line was circled. Twice. Once with ink. Once with knowing.

I heard Mira's breath, not sharp, not loud, but intentional. She wasn't asking questions. She was measuring my silence. So, I gave her what I give judges: a pause, followed by a smile not even God could cross-examine. "He always was dramatic," I said softly. "He wrote dramatics before breakfast."

Her pen didn't move, but her eyes did. Mira wasn't collecting evidence. She was collecting edits.

I closed the journal with the finality of a woman shutting a casket she never wanted open in the first place. But she wasn't done.

From her briefcase, next came the pharmacy blister. Twelve tablets dispensed. Four remained. Antihistamine, she said. Not enough to kill. But mixed with ethanol… She let the math hang like a verdict I wasn't supposed to hear yet.

I laughed. A short, deliberate breath. "He mixed whisky with everything. Pollen, panic, platforms. He self-medicated his existence."

She nodded. Then, without lifting her gaze: "Everyone knew that."

And there it was. The violence wasn't in the dosage. It was in the difference between what the world saw and what I orchestrated beneath it. I didn't flinch. Flinching is confession.

Instead, I leaned forward. Gave her strategy dressed as honesty. "Let me supply context before gossip hardens into gospel."

She uncapped her pen. Blood-red ink. "Context is free," she said. "Fabrication charges interest."

Then she asked it. The question she'd circled in her mind before I'd even walked in. "Did you love him on the final day?"

I smiled. Slow. Measured. "I loved the hush his absence was scheduled to bring."

Her eyebrow lifted one millimetre. Margin notation made.

Mira's voice stayed flat. "You also managed his finances, meal prep, and PR. He was handled, Aarti. With precision."

I exhaled slowly. Mira wasn't here for accusations. She was studying me like a case study that had walked into her office with makeup on. "You haven't accused me of anything," I said carefully.

She poured tea into both cups, unhurried. "I'm not a cop anymore," she replied. "I don't need to accuse. I just follow the narrative until it tells on itself."

I laughed, short, forced. "Narratives lie."

"Not the good ones. The good ones crack under their own symmetry." Her pen rested next to the journal, ink the colour of old blood. "Every woman buries a version of herself in marriage," Mira said softly. "You just buried him, too."

Silence. Sharp, deliberate.

"Is this an interrogation?" I asked.

"It's an observation," she corrected. "You're too neat, Aarti. Too scripted. Every timeline accounted for… except the metadata."

My pulse skipped. She knew. Not everything. Not enough to convict, but enough to unravel the curation. I stood, ready to leave, chin high. "You won't find enough to prosecute."

She smiled, a hint too sharp. "Prosecution needs proof. But public sentiment? It just needs pattern recognition."

The handshake was ritual. Cold, clean, missionary calm. Outside, a drill screamed from a child's mouth. A laugh cracked. Then silence.

In the hallway, she let it slip, not to me, but to the closing elevator doors. "Justice doesn't require confession. Just coherence. And your life?" Her eyes narrowed slightly. "A little too… edited."

I didn't flinch. I nodded. Calm. Cold. Her reflection vanished in steel. Mine remained.

*

This isn't about guilt. Guilt is too simple. This is about authorship.

Mira didn't want a conviction. She wanted the footnotes. The drafts. The metadata. And in those footnotes, my fingerprints were everywhere.

I handed her back the journal like an exhausted scholar surrendering a thesis, knowing I'd cited the devil in every line. She said nothing.

But just before I left, I heard her murmur: "She didn't break character. Not even for him."

Not suspicion. Recognition. Recognition is the real death sentence. An accusation you can fight. Recognition… stays.

And that's when I knew: I wasn't being investigated for murder. I was being studied for authorship.

*

The next morning, the news bloomed like a bruise across the nation. Not from police leaks, but from gravity. The journal had surfaced. "*Raghav's Final Warning?*", "*Widow or Architect?*", "*Mental Health or Murder Mystery?*"

One line echoed like scripture on every reel, every chyron: "*If I die peacefully, ask her why she's smiling.*"

No one mentioned my silence. But they noticed it. Silence, after all, is the sharpest tool a woman can wield when men are still holding microphones.

*

Mira wasn't coming for me with the law. She was coming with a *narrative.*

And the worst part? Not what she found. But what I hadn't destroyed. The trial wasn't coming later. It had already started.

And I was the defendant in a courtroom with no judge, just millions of jurors waiting to decide who looked more… human.

***

CHAPTER 22:
Mira Builds a Case

"The best traps don't look like cages. They look like invitations."

Not all storms arrive with thunder. Some slip in like moisture: silent, persistent, reshaping the walls before you realise you're breathing something heavier.

That's how Mira returned. Not as a detective, but as condensation. Settling into the corners of my life, seeping into the spaces I thought I'd vacuum-sealed. Unseen, unwelcome, impossible to ignore. She didn't chase me. She just… lingered.

By the time you notice her, you've already said too much. Breathed too shallow. Moved too quickly. She doesn't chase guilt. She chloroforms it gently, wraps it in linen, and waits for it to wake up and start talking on its own. I used to think the threat would come in the form of sirens. Mira proved it would come in sentence structure.

She wasn't building a charge sheet. She was building corrosion: slow, deliberate decay. The kind that doesn't scream "guilty." It whispers, *"inconsistency."*

*

She arrived without an announcement that morning. No warrant. No badge. Just that soft clinical knock that sounds more like a therapist calling time on denial.

"Thought I'd drop by. Just a few clarifications."

Casual. Practiced. No notes in hand. Which made her more dangerous than anyone who carried a file.

"Of course," I said, stepping aside. "You want tea?"

"I've already had some," she replied. But she sat anyway.

She didn't start with questions. She never did. Instead, she walked through the living room like a curator, fingers trailing against polished wood and untouched upholstery. She didn't stare at the photographs; that would be too obvious, so she studied what was absent.

"You redecorated," she noted, almost fondly.

"Fresh start," I replied. "Grief leaves fingerprints."

"And sometimes… erases them," she murmured.

Then she reached the bookshelf. She let her fingers trail across the bookshelf, each motion delicate, until they stopped at *The Art of War*. She paused. Tilted her head. Then pulled it just enough to reveal the object behind it:

A second black Moleskine. Not Raghav's. Mine. I had forgotten this one. Old. Half-full. Pre-trial. Pre-murder. My breath caught, but she didn't react.

"Interesting hiding place," she murmured. "You like strategy?"

"Every woman does," I said. "She just doesn't call it that."

She flipped through a few pages, nothing incriminating. No timestamps, no dosages, no outlines of intent. Just quotes, bullet points, post-therapy mantras.

She closed it. "You're lucky. Most people leave chaos behind. You left curation."

A compliment? No. A footnote.

*

We moved to the dining table. She didn't mention the evidence tags from last week. Didn't bring up the spreadsheet. Didn't even mention the metadata showing the deletion logged at 2:15 a.m., a full ten minutes after Raghav's body had gone still.

But I knew she knew. And she knew I knew.

She rested her palms flat on the table. "I've been studying timelines."

"And?"

"They line up."

"That's a good thing, right?"

She gave me that look. Not suspicion. Almost pity. "Too well," she said. "Like someone scripted them backwards."

I smiled. "People always call women over-prepared when we aren't visibly falling apart."

*

Then she did something unexpected. She made a mistake. She misquoted the therapist's name.

"Dr. Ahaan Joshi," she said.

"Dr. Bhatia," I corrected. Too fast. Reflex.

She blinked. Not surprised. But she let it hang long enough for me to feel like maybe, maybe, she wasn't omniscient after all.

"Right," she said lightly. "Bhatia. The *chai* guy."

She picked up her pen again, clicked it once. Red ink. Same as always. But now, it looked deliberate. Final. Three missing appointments. No reasons. No notes. Just gaps, like teeth lost in a smile you suddenly don't trust.

And just like that, she exposed the therapy records for what they really were: branded damage control.

I didn't defend them. I didn't need to. Because women like Mira don't demand explanations. They document patterns.

*

I offered her more tea. She declined with a softness that could slice arteries. Her voice, low, thoughtful, dressed in velvet but sharpened at the edges, floated across the table: "Do you believe people can kill without hating?"

I froze. Not visibly. But my hand tightened around the cup just once, porcelain against bone. "Yes," I said. Smooth. Like lying in silk gloves. "Sometimes," I added, "it's the only ethical way to finish something."

She nodded. Not with approval. Not suspicion. *Recognition.*

Recognition is always worse. Accusations can be denied. But recognition? That stays.

*

The silence stretched until I broke it.

"Is this a formal inquiry?"

"Not yet," she said. "We're still in… narrative phase."

"So, I'm not a suspect."

"You're not a criminal," she said softly. "You're a case."

My spine straightened. "There's no evidence."

"Not of murder," she said. "But grief?" She tilted her head. "Grief leaves fingerprints. And yours are too symmetrical."

She stood and sat across from me like a question I hadn't dared to ask myself. Her notebook was open. Still the same red ink. Red, not for drama. Red for edits. Red for contradictions circled in silence.

She didn't build cases. She built frameworks. Not trials. Timelines.

*

Her hand hovered over the page for a moment before she said, almost to herself: "He didn't fear your cruelty. He feared your mercy."

It took me a second to realise what she meant. Because cruelty leaves a trace. Mercy doesn't. Mercy is cleaner, colder. The kill that feels like a hug.

*

She stood to leave. Not abruptly. Smoothed her *kurta*. She didn't need dramatics. But at the threshold, she turned slightly. Voice low. Calm. Too calm. "You've built a beautiful version of grief," she said. "But good fiction always cracks at the second act."

"I didn't write fiction," I said.

"No," she nodded. "But you edited."

And in that moment, I knew: She wasn't holding a case file. She was holding my manuscript. And she was revising. In red. Then, just before leaving, she capped the pen and smiled. Not with victory, but with alignment. Like two writers finishing the same sentence from opposite ends of the page.

Only after she was gone did I realise: She'd taken the second Moleskine with her. Not as evidence. As a test. And I'd passed. Or failed. I didn't know which.

But the worst part? She hadn't accused me. She'd left me room to explain.

Which meant she was building something far worse than a case. She was building a stage. The story wasn't being told. It was being rewritten.

And I wasn't sure if I was the author, or just… a character under revision.

***

PART *Four*

THE TRIAL OF THE CALM WIFE

CHAPTER 23: Legal Camouflage

"The system wasn't built to protect women like me. That's why I taught myself how to pilot it better than anyone else."

I filed it on a Monday. Because Mondays are not days, they're declarations. Mondays are for offence disguised as documentation. And I knew what I was doing. I wasn't submitting a complaint. I was constructing a weapon. With formatting.

I didn't carry anger into the advocate's office that morning. Anger is too emotional, too loud, too easy to dismiss as hysteria when worn by a woman with neat hair and quieter eyes. No, what I carried was a blueprint of architecture disguised as grievance. And the scent of jasmine still clung to my scarf, always the scent of innocence, curated.

*

Subject Line: Notice of Intent to Initiate Legal Action: Defamation, Harassment of Grieving Widow, Violation of Privacy Norms.

That last phrase wasn't for the law. That was for optics.

Privacy norms: A phrase that makes even bureaucrats recoil like schoolboys caught reading a woman's diary. It's not legal. It's a linguistic landmine.

The email was sent at 9:02 a.m. Never on the hour. That would seem rehearsed. Precision signals purpose. Subtlety signals control.

I addressed it to the Deputy Commissioner of Police and the Foundation's Legal Compliance Cell. For courtesy, not confession.

I copied two journalists—both of whom still used "intersectional" like it was a seasonal trend—and one editor who had once posted #MeToo in lowercase italics, as if rebellion should be font-sensitive. I added one more: a softly spoken media woman in Mumbai known not for writing about abuse, but for collecting survivors like postcards—neatly arranged, quietly shelved, and selectively displayed.

The only attachment was a ₹5,00,000 donation receipt to The Raghav Kapoor Foundation for Men's Mental Health. No apology. No footnote of remorse. Just the receipt. Because guilt doesn't move public opinion. But philanthropy? That's the clickbait of compassion.

*

By noon, *sympathy was trending*. Not for Mira. For me.

They posted my photograph from the vigil, the one where my eyes looked like grief dipped in candlelight. No one asked for my side. They simply constructed it for me.

And this—this—is where women like Mira lose. Not because they're wrong, but because they still believe truth has currency in public trials. I don't trade in truth. I trade in *structure*.

Mira received notice from the CP office three days later. The internal memo was dressed like concern, but smelled like political euthanasia:

Notice: Cease Communication

From: Office of the Commissioner of Police

To: Ms. Mira Rao

Subject: Unauthorised Contact with Investigative Subject: Mrs. Aarti Kapoor

You are hereby instructed to **immediately cease all direct or indirect communication** *with Mrs. Aarti Kapoor, effective upon receipt of this notice. Any further contact shall be considered a* **violation of protocol** *and subject to legal review.*

This directive is issued in view of your **unauthorised involvement** *and increasing* **emotional proximity** *to a sensitive subject during an ongoing civil recovery period.*

This matter is considered closed.

Do not reopen it.

*

I watched the video of her leaving the building. She didn't look back, didn't blink, didn't shrink. She just walked, jaw clenched, shoulders like iron latticework, past the sea of cameras. No sunglasses. No badge flourish. Only that unkillable dignity. The kind that doesn't fade even when the system tries to pixelate it.

I muted the volume because I already knew the anchors' script. "Why was she pulled?", "What did she uncover?"

They always ask the wrong questions. Women like Mira don't get removed for being *wrong*. They get removed for being *early*.

*

And then came the envelope. No courier, no postage. Just my name, written like a whisper on the front. Inside was a photocopy of Raghav's journal. That line again: *"If I die peacefully, ask her why she's smiling."*

Only this time, it was underlined in graphite. And below it was a familiar scrawl in red ink. Mira's handwriting. No signature. No threat. Just intent. The kind of quiet reminder that doesn't scream, "I see you." It just says, "You forgot to delete me."

I didn't flinch. Not because I wasn't startled, but because I had trained my breath to treat revelation like liturgy. When the divine enters, you don't scream. You bow.

*

The call came at 12:11 p.m. Because Mira was surgical with time. There was no hello, no intro. Just a breath, and that impossible voice that sounds like someone who has already accepted the weight of everyone's sins.

"You're good," she said.

I didn't thank her, nor did I gloat. I let the sentence hang between us like a blade suspended by piano wire. "I'm tired of playing fair," I finally said. Not dramatic. Not regretful. Just... ready.

She didn't reply. Because she doesn't do dialogue. She does *tension.* And that's what we sat in. Two women, tethered to a crime no court would fully understand. One chasing justice, one drafting legacy.

Then, her voice came again, low, measured, like closing a confession box. "This won't make you innocent."

I smiled. "I'm not after innocence," I said. "I'm after copyright."

There it was: the full admission. Not guilt. Not regret. Because I didn't want absolution. I didn't kill for freedom. I wanted authorship. People don't care who writes history, only who signs it. I was both.

Her exhale was soft. Almost... entertained. "Congratulations. You'll walk free. But you'll never be clean."

I didn't deny it. I didn't have to. "I already did."

And we both knew what that meant. Not legally. Philosophically.

She didn't hang up. Of course, she didn't. The most dangerous conversations don't end neatly. They hang like unfinished edits on a manuscript you don't want to revise but can't publish yet.

The system hadn't protected me. Not really. Systems don't protect sharp women. They protect dull men. But I didn't need protection. I needed precedent. And I was writing mine in the footnotes of other people's grief.

The call ended with both of us breathing. It wasn't a victory; it was an acknowledgement. Respect among killers. One with paperwork, one with memory.

And Mira? She wasn't chasing charges anymore. She was writing her own closing arguments. Not for court, but for history. Because that's the real trial, and we were both winning. Just in different fonts.

*

In the end, the system didn't rescue me. It handed me the chisel. And I carved my face into the stone walls they tried to cage me in. Smiling. Always smiling. Because survival isn't enough. Legacy is.

And Mira? She won't bury me. She didn't lose. She could scratch her red ink against margins as much as she wanted.

***

CHAPTER 24:
The Netflix Trap

"When the world lines up to narrate your story, it's not about truth. It's about who gets the royalties."

It didn't start with a press release. It started with a deck. Black cover, soft matte finish. A production house I'd never heard of, but whose partners I knew in footnotes. Their films didn't make headlines, but they made murmurs. Festival credits. Jury mentions. Documentaries with names like *Unsilenced* and *The Women We Forgot.* No big stars. Just slow shots of ruined buildings and women smoking at window sills. The kind of cinema that pretends it hates exploitation while monetising empathy frame by frame.

They never call it what it is. Not exploitation, not commodification, certainly not extraction.

They call it *interest. A Limited Docu-Series: The Calm Widow. Six Episodes. Global Distribution. Creative Control… negotiable.* "*Crafted with sensitivity and nuance.*" But I've learned that the word *nuance* is just how art people apologise for betrayal in high definition.

I ran my finger down the list of credits: Series Creator: Tara D'Souza. Of course.

I had read her before. Not her films, but her *articles*. Before she became *streamable*, she was the journalist who dismantled men in column inches while smiling through interviews. The kind of writer who could expose corruption and then fly under the radar because she never used adjectives, only verbs. The same Tara who once wrote an award-winning piece on female incarceration and then posted a selfie outside Tihar Jail.

A few days later, Tara D'Souza showed up at my door. I opened the door. She smiled. Polite but not overly familiar. No camera crew, no entourage. Just her, calm, well-dressed, efficient. She didn't introduce herself like someone famous, though she was, in her own niche way.

"Thank you for having me," she said, stepping in like someone who had done this before, many times.

We sat in the living room. No small talk. Just an open leather folder on her lap and a long look at me, not judging, just scanning.

"I'm not here to sensationalise," she began. "We want to create something thoughtful. With care. With honesty."

I nodded cautiously.

She continued, "We're developing a limited series of six episodes, centred around women whose narratives have been... taken from them. We think your story matters."

I didn't say anything. Just listened.

"I know this is personal," she added. "We're not looking to dissect your trauma. We want to understand how you lived through it. How you came out of it."

I offered her tea. Darjeeling. No sugar. She accepted. The silence that followed wasn't awkward; it was calculated. She wanted me to speak first. I didn't.

So, she shifted her approach. "You're not a victim in our version," she said. "You're the centre. The voice. The truth."

I looked at her. "Do I get to decide what version that is?"

She smiled faintly. "We'd love for you to be involved. We want your approval on the arc, the tone. This isn't true crime. It's... a reckoning."

A reckoning. That word again. I leaned back. "Let's be honest. You're here because people didn't like how I handled Raghav's death. Because I didn't cry enough. Because I didn't perform grief the right way."

Tara didn't deny it. Instead, she said, "People are uncomfortable when women don't break."

I could've laughed. But I didn't. She slid a thin deck across the table. Sample episode titles. Visual references. Mood boards. It looked clean, polished. Cold.

"There's one scene we're exploring," she said, eyes on me. "A window shot. Silhouette. Not literal, of course. Just a way to show... isolation."

I didn't react.

"Do I die in the end?" I asked.

She blinked. Then smiled. "Not physically."

I nodded.

This wasn't about honouring anyone. Not Raghav. Not me. It was about getting the green light. Streaming rights. Global appeal. They wanted a woman who looked put-together and sounded broken.

Tara sat across from me, rolling a fountain pen between her fingers. "I don't believe in villains," she said.

I nodded. "Neither do I."

She tilted her head. "But I do believe in *patterns*. And your interviews… they're… very well-rehearsed."

It wasn't an accusation. It was *foreplay*. That's when she pulled out her final act surprise like a magician pretending like she hadn't been prepping the trick all along.

"When we were granted access to Raghav's phone backups… we found something curious. A folder."

I knew this part already. Mira's fingerprints were still wet on this narrative. Tara smiled like a good detective in soft lighting. "Password-protected," she said.

Of course.

She let the pause sit there like a cigarette burning unattended.

"What do you think was inside?"

I blinked, long and slow, like a woman who still remembered classical dance training but no longer performed. She looked at me like a priest waiting for my sins to confess themselves. I sipped my tea. "I don't chase ghosts," I said. "And I don't break into letters meant for someone else."

It wasn't a denial. It was a sentence made of steel and velvet.

Her eyes flicked once, with the briefest flare of disappointment. Because Tara didn't want the truth, she wanted a collapse. And I was still upright. She studied me. Waiting for a slip. Waiting for a twitch of the mouth or a knuckle that cracked involuntarily. Nothing.

That's the thing with women like me: We don't flinch. We redact.

She didn't push. She just smiled, packed her notes neatly, and said the most dangerous sentence a filmmaker can offer a woman like me: "We'll send you the draft script when we're ready. We want your voice in this."

They always want your voice when they can't find your fingerprints. But it was never my voice she wanted. It was my confession in lowercase.

Lisa's eyes never met mine that day. Whether she was Mira's pawn or just an overpaid spectator, I'd never know. But she didn't warn me. That was enough.

*

That night, I watched two episodes of her last docuseries. The cinematography was gorgeous. Warm. Feminist. Empowering.

sThe heroine was a single mother who exposed a local politician's corruption ring and won a national bravery award. The real story? The mother lost custody of her child three years later. They never covered that part.

That's when I realised: the story was never about *justice*. Because Tara doesn't tell stories. She edits consequences. It was about *framing*. And Tara was here for my frame, not my freedom. But the cameras? They don't know yet.

By the time Netflix gets to post-production, I'll already have written the alternate ending.

*

Tara texted a follow-up by noon. "We can co-produce your memoir adaptation. Full creative sign-off."

I wrote back only one line: "I'll send you the draft after publication. Until then, no unauthorised filming."

They thought they were adapting *me*. But I had already written the ending.

And Tara? She doesn't realise she's already a character in my next project. She just hasn't read the script yet. I didn't kill Raghav because I was angry. I killed him because I was bored with unfinished stories. Now I'm finishing all of them myself. Credits optional. And Mira? She's not gone; she's just off-screen, waiting for her return arc.

Raghav's ghost would keep haunting hashtags, and Mira would keep chasing the missing lines between my smiles. But the ending? That was now in my hands.

This wasn't a true crime tale. It was a limited series, memoir, and public redemption story, and I had already secured the executive producer credit.

Some women rot under judgment. I negotiated the screenplay.

***

CHAPTER 25: Trial Announcement

"It was never about proving murder. It was about proving I didn't cry correctly."

The petition arrived in a white envelope that reeked of bureaucratic perfume: crisp, cold, and dangerous. A landmine dressed in etiquette. Delhi High Court letterhead. Black ink, blue signature. Like someone had taken the time to detonate politely.

Filed by Kamini Kapoor. Raghav's mother. Matriarch. Mausoleum. A woman who wore widowhood like a veil and vengeance like vermillion. She had once told me, smiling with a mouth full of salt, *"A good daughter-in-law doesn't argue. She edits her personality."* Now she'd filed her final edit.

And because venom always comes with garnish, she'd slipped in an eviction clause. As if my home was just another trinket from her son's life to be repossessed. Buried in legal jargon were two sharp truths: She wanted me accused of murder. And evicted from the home I once shared with her son.

She cited everything: conspiracy, destruction of evidence, and harassment. Even invoked a senior citizen protection clause, because irony is best served in court.

But I knew this wasn't about justice. It was about legacy. It was a mother who couldn't accept that her son's downfall came from within, not beside.

And in her eyes, grief wasn't grief unless it had a villain.

*

She chose me. She had weaponised it to exhume her son. It wasn't the law that made me grip the pages until they crumpled. It was the precision of it. She knew exactly where to cut.

The accusation wasn't loud. It didn't need to be. It was precise. *"Grief behaviour inconsistent with ordinary Hindu widowhood," "Premeditated emotional detachment," "Probable financial motive concealed behind 'curated mourning'," "Grief patterns inconsistent with expected sociocultural behaviour."*

Translation? She didn't cry right. She smiled too early. She grieved like she'd rehearsed. That would've been amusing if it weren't... architecture.

Attached was a spreadsheet. I opened it on my phone at the Foundation's café, surrounded by interns hashtagging feminism into oblivion. The file name? "Timeline_Collapse.xlsx."

Except… it wasn't mine. Raghav's name was stamped across the metadata. His morbid foresight was encoded in cells and formulas. There were tabs like chapters: Method. Risk. Narrative Leverage. Contingencies.

Midway through, a line blinked up at me like a severed nerve: "*If public mourning fails, make her the plot.*"

He had drafted his death like a cinematic thesis. And worse? He had anticipated my writing the sequel.

It wasn't a suicide. It wasn't a murder. It was a screenplay. Two writers, same genre, different endings.

Only now, the court had found his draft. And they were preparing to adapt.

The media latched on like termites to polished wood. *NDTV* framed it as feminist dissonance. *Zee* called it "*India's* Gone Girl." Instagram reels narrated my facial expressions. My lipstick became a plot device. My Spotify playlist was cited in speculative threads.#WidowOrWriter, #TrialByTandooriGrief, #JusticeForRaghav. One influencer recreated my funeral look. Caption: *"Signs your friend might be Aarti Kapoor."* I didn't report her. I archived it under a folder titled: *Artefacts of Digital Misogyny.*

Then came Mira; not at my door, but at my threshold.

She arrived unannounced, standing on my balcony like a quiet threat. Not a detective anymore, just a woman refusing to blink while the world overdosed on headlines.

Her words were steel wrapped in civility: "You have forty-eight hours before the court admits the charges," "This isn't about guilt anymore. It's about authorship," "Submit your version… or someone else writes it for you."

I didn't offer her tea. I didn't offer her lies. I offered her silence.

Mira's smile was cold. "Silence works in grief. Not in courtrooms."

Then she left, leaving a USB drive on my table, like a loaded weapon I didn't request. Inside were audio backups, memos, and therapy notes. Some were real. Some were strategically misplaced.

I called Reva Narayan, and that night she arrived; not like a lawyer, but like the courtroom's muscle memory, sharp, practised, inevitable. rey khadi *kurta.* Unbrushed hair. The kind of woman who could argue constitutional law while folding her *dupatta* like a threat.

Her greeting wasn't a hello. It was an assessment. "You're still calm. Good. Panic is for people who lose cases. We're here to make case law."

We sat in my old study. My guilt, stacked quietly in the corners, gathering dust like obsolete doctrine. I handed her everything. Not the murder. The architecture. The calendar invites, the therapy bills, the blank pages of my grief. The ones I left untouched on purpose.

She listened without interruption, scribbled nothing, just watched the air calcify.

Then said it, so plainly it burned: "We're not selling innocence. We're selling inevitability."

I paused. "You mean... I'm not defending myself?"

She pushed her glasses up. "They aren't accusing you of murder. They're accusing you of emotional fraud." She didn't blink when she added, "We don't deny curation. We reframe it as a strategy. Grief management, not concealment. You weren't cold. You were conditioned."

In a single sentence, she had sliced through decades of cultural gaslighting and handed me a closing argument soaked in theory and blood.

In my old study, surrounded by the skeletal remains of my marriage, Reva dissected every allegation. Not with sympathy, but with scalpel-like precision.

"They'll bury you under Section 302, unless we make it medically implausible," she said bluntly. "Section 120B needs proof of collusion, which they don't have. We torch that with a timeline matrix. "Section 201 hinges on deleted data; we convert that into privacy violation counter-litigation. And the Senior Citizens Act?" Her smile turned predatory. "We recast it—you weren't harassing an elderly woman; you were safeguarding against financial misappropriation by the deceased. Your composure? Expertwitness psychologists will testify it's a traumaresponse, not *mens rea*. We don't scream innocence. We whisper inevitability."

Because women like me? We are the thesis statements in men's posthumous autobiographies. We don't get the final word. We become the word limit.

*

Reva laid it out: This wouldn't be a trial for murder. It would be a referendum on the criminalisation of female stillness.

"Your crime isn't homicide," she said. "It's refusing to collapse when society demanded it."

I watched her walk out, *dupatta* brushing the floor like a closing gavel, and I knew: this wasn't going to end with acquittal. It would end with an annotation.

*

That night, in front of the mirror, I rehearsed. Not the lie. The stillness.

"I didn't kill Raghav because I hated him. I killed him because the world only listens to women once we stop explaining."

The trial isn't about truth. It's about tone. And I've always known how to pitch my voice for a guilty nation that wants a grieving woman to apologise for surviving too well.

Let them call it a trial, I call it a publication. My final draft was to be footnoted in silence, typeset in restraint, and copyrighted with blood. The trial wouldn't be fought in that courtroom. It would be fought in every living room, every WhatsApp thread, every social media poll asking, "Do you believe her?"

They weren't trying to convict me. They were trying to *caption* me. And captions always win. *"I wasn't the perfect wife. But I was the perfect prototype of what makes India suspicious: a woman too composed to be pitied."*

***

CHAPTER 26:
The Trial That Wasn't

"They didn't acquit me. They just ran out of vocabulary for my kind of guilt."

There is no silence like courtroom silence in an Indian summer. The kind where ceiling fans creak like old confessions, where filtered water tastes like paperwork, and where grief becomes something you sweat through your spine, not your eyes.

They didn't title it *State vs. Aarti Kapoor.* That would've been honest. Instead, the cause list read: "In Re: Verification of Anomalous Circumstances Surrounding the Demise of Raghav Kapoor (CRL WP 1136/2025)".

A title designed not to accuse, but to allow room for discomfort. Because discomfort is safer than indictment. Discomfort can be televised.

The room was packed. Lawyers in half-sleeved formals, journalists rehearsing outrage in their notebooks, one influencer in a chiffon saree, whispering legal jargon into a lav mic for a reel she hadn't filmed yet, and me, perfectly still. Not innocent. Just inevitable.

The Prosecution, Mr. Jain, opened first. He wore a tailored black suit and the smug lean of a man who pre-savours convictions. His voice was measured, his gait smug. The kind of man who thinks a court is a TED Talk with better acoustics.

"Your Honour," he began, "this is not a murder trial. Not officially. But it is a case of *unnatural absence.* Of grief that didn't cry loudly enough. Of a widow who rehearsed composure with such discipline, she became a suspect in her own tragedy."

He pointed to the screen. A slideshow. Not of evidence, but of timelines. Emails, metadata, and smiling photographs where Raghav's eyes looked like they'd seen something ahead of time.

"She is not being accused because she didn't love her husband," he said, his voice tightening.

"This is an inquiry into a cultural betrayal, a widow who dismembered tradition before her husband's body cooled."

Murmurs followed. Not legal ones. Spectator ones. And that's the real court in this country: the gallery. He ended with what he thought was literary flair: "She may not have pulled the trigger, but she loaded the script."

*

Reva Narayan Rose. Not like the opposition. Like inevitability. The kind of lawyer who doesn't stand. She manifests. *FabIndia* khadi. Half-moon spectacles. A woman who looks like she buried the Constitution under her pillow for twenty years and can quote the Preamble in four languages. Her voice was low and clear, designed for moral injury.

"Milords," she said quietly, "this case is built on the prosecution's inability to tolerate female restraint."

Jain objected. She didn't flinch.

"We are defending a woman prosecuted for having control over her own emotions—a non-cognizable offence, last I checked."

She spoke like democracy had hand-written her cross-examinations.

"We are not denying that my client didn't cry the way television demands," she said.

"We're stating that she had no reason to audition for a nation that rewards wailing and punishes intelligence."

The judge blinked. Once. Slowly. Reva turned to the gallery. "Grief in women is not trusted unless it bleeds. Aarti Kapoor did not bleed. She bled before you ever saw her. In silence, in spreadsheets, in all the ways this country has taught its women to prepare for their own trials—not in court, but in living rooms. Grief isn't evidence. Emotional choreography isn't guilt."

She introduced psychologist testimonies, cultural studies, and expert witnesses who spoke of "adaptive dissociation" and "functional grief."

"Women in India survive by discipline," Reva said. "My client's crime was surviving *well*." She paused, perfectly, and then delivered the line like a verdict: Her cross-reference of Section 302 IPC was brutal. "No physical evidence. Post-mortem inconclusive. The autopsy report doesn't establish external injury or forced ingestion.

"Under Section 120B IPC, conspiracy requires two or more people. The prosecution hasn't produced one verifiable co-conspirator. On Section 201 IPC, concealment requires proof of intentional suppression. Instead, they present a structured life schedule and call it a cover-up." She slid in a case law citation like a dagger: "State of Haryana vs Bhajan Lal (1992), where malicious proceedings under the pretext of investigation were quashed at the threshold."

Her focus turned to the widowhood eviction claim under Section 24 of the Maintenance and Welfare of Parents and Senior Citizens Act, 2007.

Reva's voice sharpened. "It is a grotesque misuse of welfare legislation to evict a widow from her matrimonial home because she's deemed insufficiently broken."

She continued after a small pause, "She didn't kill Raghav Kapoor. She killed the idea that wives must be emotionally consumable in order to be believable."

*

They called Mira Rao first. Once removed from the investigation, now summoned as a reluctant expert. They called her a "*Behavioural Observer*," which is courtroom language for: the woman whose opinion hurts the most. She wore a navy blue cotton *saree*, along with no jewellery and no emotions. Just Mira Rao: the woman who doesn't speak in conclusions. Only footnotes with fangs.

When Mira took her oath, she didn't close her eyes or bow her head. She just looked straight at the judge and said, "I do," like someone confirming that rain falls down, not up.

Her testimony wasn't emotional. That would've been beneath her. No trembling. No grand narratives of justice. Just sentences stripped of adverbs, like bullets polished with grammar. Her testimony was academic violence. Calm. Clean. Brutal.

"Mrs. Kapoor's affect displayed systematic regulation. Not criminal intent, not psychopathy, but a controlled detachment cultivated through years of adaptive social conditioning."

Mr. Jain interrupted. "Are you calling her manipulative?"

Mira didn't blink. "I'm calling her adapted."

The gallery stilled. She laid out each observation like cold-cut evidence on fine china: "Mrs. Kapoor displayed emotional patterns inconsistent with normative spousal loss. Her grief was rehearsed. Her language, formalised. Her affect was muted. Her empathy was structured. Her mourning was curated. Her pauses were rhythmic, her syntax shifted from active to passive when recounting her husband's final days.

"She has not referred to him by name once in this court. She speaks like a woman who doesn't mourn in decibels. She pauses like a woman trained to make grief look like grammar."

The judge leaned forward. The reporters scribbled like they'd just heard God clear his throat. Mira folded her hands and looked at me. Not with accusation, but with recognition.

She doesn't say I'm guilty. She says I'm distant, detached, disciplined. Dangerous in a way the law hasn't yet defined. And in that moment, I realised: she wasn't here to indict me. She was here to prove that there was no law yet for my kind.

What stunning precision, I thought. *I should compliment her vocabulary after this is over.*

Not sarcastically, but genuinely. Because Mira didn't accuse. She translated what I had kept in encrypted silences. And that's the deadliest kind of testimony. There was no section in the IPC for being "too composed while grieving." And yet here we were.

And then, it was my turn. I wore white khadi, handwoven, national, rough enough to mourn in and stiff enough to say: *I understand the weight of tradition.* There was a black thread around my wrist: widowhood, not fashion.

I took the stand with the gait of someone who's done this before, not in court, but in kitchens. Where silence is performance. Where grief is kneaded into *rotis.*

When asked to speak, I do. Gently. Precisely. Not tearful. Not defiant. Just... real enough to read as pain. I spoke in the tone I'd practised before a thousand bathroom mirrors: not victim, not villain, just someone who's been left behind by both God and breakfast.

"My husband," I began, "was a good man in the way good men are defined in this country.

Ambitious. Smiling. Loud in social settings. Quiet in personal ones."

I described his insomnia, his carefully curated breakdowns, his digital archive of moods, Google Calendar entries that sounded like diary confessions, and yes, the spreadsheet.

But I didn't cry. I didn't wail. I said, "Women in my family didn't cry in public. They served tea. They served composure. They served dinner after miscarriages and folded *sarees* after funerals.

"My grief was formatted," I said. "Because women like me are only believed when our grief is spell-checked."

Jain sneered, "You profited from his death."

I smiled faintly. "No, Counsel. I survived it."

The judge interrupted sharply, "Please stick to the facts. This isn't a literary trial."

I didn't raise my voice. That's for men. I didn't beg. That's for amateurs. I let one tear fall. Just one. Right eye. Timed. No smudge. That's the acceptable metric. More than one was manipulative. Less meant you were a sociopath.

Reva closed the day. Her voice didn't rise. It anchored. "My client isn't here because she failed her husband. She's here because she failed your expectations. This isn't a murder trial.

It's a test of aesthetic obedience."

She looked at the judge. "Mrs. Kapoor did not cry enough to satisfy collective doubt. But I ask the court, when did we start convicting women for surviving *stylishly*? My client was humiliated online, gaslit in silence, and rewritten by a man celebrated for his cruelty."

She called it: *emotional coercion, narrative domination,* and *grief rebranded by patriarchy*. She quoted Article 21 like it's a love letter to forgotten wives.

"She's not a sociopath. She's just a woman who speaks in complete sentences. And this country is not used to that."

The gallery rustled. Someone's *dupatta* shifted. Someone else coughed guilt into their sleeve.

"We're not here to deny the grief was curated," she said. "We are here to argue—it had to be. Because when women scream, they're hysterical. And when they don't? They're called murderers."

The judge didn't interrupt. Not once. And me? I watched the gavel rise like a breath. They were trying to explain me, and failing. Because there's no section in the Indian Penal Code for "too elegant while grieving."

Just whispers. Just documentaries. Just history, footnoted in red ink.

They didn't convict me. They translated me poorly. Because I wasn't on trial. The definition of guilt was. And I had already edited it. Footnote by footnote. In my own font.

***

CHAPTER 27:
The Science of Suggestion

"Facts don't win trials. Narratives do."

It wasn't the prosecution's cross-examination that scratched at my skin—it was the screen behind them. *Serum Toxicology Report No. 0982/MH/2025. Forensic Exhibit P-17: Toxicological Profile of Deceased, Raghav Kapoor.*

They brought a forensic pathologist to read my life like it was a lab result. Not to confirm death, but to provoke discomfort. And, I was seated in the centre of an amphitheatre disguised as justice, while Mumbai humidity curled through the ceiling fans like someone eavesdropping on sin.

Dr. Praveen Kripalani. Author. Lecturer. Man of impeccable ties and imperfect truths. The kind of witness who speaks in decimals, not doubts. He walked in like a man entering an operating theatre, not a courtroom. Surgical. Clean.

The judge shifted forward in his chair the way men do when they already think they know the answer but want it said aloud anyway. Praveen didn't speak like a witness. He spoke like a lecturer who already knew half the students in the room were going to fail.

His testimony had the slow elegance of a scalpel: sharp, without speed. "In my opinion," he began, adjusting the mic with surgeon's detachment, "the levels of benzodiazepine derivatives found in Mr. Raghav Kapoor's system… cannot be explained by over-the-counter medications.

"Your Honour, the postmortem toxicology revealed clonazepam metabolite at 212 ng/mL—triple the safe range."

No emotional inflexion. Just numbers.

"Additionally, liver tissue exhibited cumulative deposition of benzodiazepine residues, consistent with chronic administration exceeding safe pharmacological thresholds. Specifically, over a minimum of 40 days, culminating in acute cardiopulmonary suppression."

The room froze; not from outrage, but the mechanical terror of clinical precision.

He moved to slides: coloured assays, plasma reports, hepatic distribution maps. "Death was consistent with mixed benzodiazepine toxicity, complicated by pre-existing mild fatty liver infiltration, making metabolism slower, toxicity faster."

No screaming. No blunt force trauma. Just a man extinguished in slow gradients of chemical silence.

The prosecutor rose smugly: "Doctor, could this be administered unnoticed in small doses, via routine food and drink?"

Kripalani's glasses glinted beneath the LED light. "Highly probable. Benzodiazepines, especially unregulated analogues, are lipophilic, binding seamlessly with fatty substrates like ghee, oil-based curries… or even protein shakes."

My fingers stayed still on my lap. I had done my homework far too well. The screen flickered behind him. Graph. Gradient blue. No jagged peaks. No sudden jumps. Just a gentle slope, the kind that kills over time, like loneliness or routine.

"Note the progression," he said, pointer hovering like a priest at a corpse. "This suggests... intentional gradual exposure over a prolonged period. Possibly administered via ingestibles. Possibly masked as exhaustion.

"At the right moment, during emotional stress or elevated heart rate—" He paused. "The heart... could stop. No bruises. No marks. Just… silence."

No fire. Just fog. The courtroom held its breath. Because, unlike murder, which screams, this suggested something worse. Planning. Whispers broke in the gallery. Words like *"slow poisoning"* and *"spousal manipulation"* slid between benches like insects beneath a shrine.

And me? I didn't blink. Because this testimony? I wrote it. Before he ever arrived. I wrote it in the margins of grocery lists, in dosage math between spoonfuls of lentils. I choreographed this arc with the patience of an architect designing a house meant to collapse, slowly, beautifully. But even architects miss a beam.

Mira Rao. Second row. No notebook. Just her gaze, unflickering. The look of a woman watching a controlled demolition she'd already mapped in her mind. She wasn't reacting to the graph. She was studying me. Because the graph was just evidence. But I? I was theatre.

And Mira? She had become the critic, not the investigator.

Reva Narayan rose for cross-questioning like someone who doesn't interrupt, just rewrites. Her linen was folded with courtroom precision. No drama. Just grammar that cuts.

"Doctor," she began softly, "do you consider yourself a pathologist... or a data interpreter?"

The courtroom blinked. So did Dr. Kripalani. "I—both, I suppose."

"Good," Reva said, almost kindly. "Does science ever deal in certainties?"

The question was harmless. Almost flattery. Praveen blinked, the way educated men blink when someone unexpected has shown up in their living room with matching vocabulary.

"Not in behavioural patterns, no," Praveen answered.

"Good," Reva Narayan said softly. "Then let's behave like scientists."

She stepped forward. Raised one exhibit: an invoice, printed on thick paper, official in a way that smells like ink has ancestry.

"Let's stay simple. Could any of these metabolites appear due to anti-anxiety or over-the-counter medication?"

"Technically... yes."

"Doctor, for the record, which Schedule under the Narcotic Drugs and Psychotropic Substances Act, 1985, regulates clonazepam?"

"Schedule H-1, Ma'am."

"Correct. And without a prescription?"

"Illegal to procure."

"But possible?"

"Yes, through unlicensed online vendors."

"And did Mr. Raghav Kapoor have a prescription for any such medication?"

"No."

"Any known mental health diagnoses?"

"None officially recorded."

She nodded. "And yet... three weeks prior to his death, he purchased unregulated clonazepam analogues. Online. Using his own email. Shipped directly to his apartment."

She held the invoice like a prayer. Offered it to the court.

"Exhibit D-42. *SleepRest Solutions*, flagged by NCB in 2023. Orders were traced to Raghav Kapoor's residence under his credentials. Multiple packages, three separate chemical derivatives of clonazepam, including Etizolam, which metabolises similarly but isn't regulated identically."

The prosecutor stiffened. Journalists adjusted their lenses. One reporter gasped audibly—amateur mistake.

"Could this substance... produce the pattern you described?" she asked, gesturing casually to the graph still hovering in the air behind him.

Dr. Kripalani hesitated. That flicker? That single microsecond of intellectual humility? That was the crack.

"In theory... yes. It's... plausible."

Not probable. Plausible. Just enough oxygen for doubt to breed.

Reva didn't gloat. She anchored. "So, to clarify for the court, what you describe is suggestive, not conclusive?"

"Correct."

"In simpler words: you cannot rule out self-induced toxaemia."

"I cannot."

The prosecutor tried to object. The judge raised a hand. The gallery murmured, uncertainty rippling like static electricity.

She didn't press harder. That's Reva's genius. She doesn't hammer. She unthreads. "Thank you, Doctor," she said, voice silk-wrapped steel. "The science has spoken. It suggests. But suggestion is not law."

The courtroom felt… looser after that. The judge leaned back. The stenographer unclenched her pen. Even the ceiling fan seemed less sure of itself. And Mira? She still hadn't blinked. Because she understood what I now did: This wasn't a war of science. It was a war of grammar. She wasn't fighting for conviction; she was building discomfort.

That was the brilliance I hadn't accounted for. I had calculated sedative dosages, timestamps, digital trails, browser wipes, calibrated tear angles for profile shots, and the optimal fabric weight for widow *sarees* in June.

But I had not accounted for a woman who was playing narrative not as law, but as entropy.

I knew from the start this would be the crack. Not blood, not bruises, but chemistry. And chemistry, like grief, is easier to misinterpret than prove. I had chosen the method precisely for this reason. A sedative whose trail could be confused with exhaustion, stress, or self-neglect. A chemical fog. And the one holding the flashlight? Controls the story.

Reva held it today, barely, but enough. And this was entropy: a room no longer sure of itself. The jury wasn't nodding anymore. They were *thinking*. That's more dangerous than rage. Rage is predictable. Thought? Thought leaks into follow-up questions, into delayed coffee shop conversations, into Reddit threads that live forever.

Even science, under oath, had been reduced to suggestion. And suggestion? That's my language. I didn't learn it from grief. I learned it from watching men lie at dinner parties.

Reva's closing that day was cold steel in silk. "Science doesn't convict. It advises. The prosecution seeks to criminalise possibility, not proof. The Indian Evidence Act, Section 101, places a burden on the prosecution. Speculation fails the threshold of proof beyond a reasonable doubt.

"My client didn't stand to gain from Raghav Kapoor's death. She inherited scrutiny, not security." She shifted toward the forensic chart. "What these curves show is death. What they fail to show is intent."

And intent—not presence of toxins—made the difference between a widow and a murderer.

When the session adjourned, I could hear the courtroom exhale. The sound of a public recalibrating its certainty. Because the truth had been moved from conviction to suggestion. And in that small shift? I survived.

*

Mira walked past me as the court emptied. Close enough for breath, far enough for law. No words, just that stare. The stare that said: *I know what you did.* The stare that meant: *And I might still be writing about it.*

And me? I smiled. Because the thing about forensic truth is: it can't interpret intention. And neither can she.

At least, not yet.

They brought in science to kill my story. But suggestion? That's a language I spoke fluently, long before I ever picked up the poison.

***

CHAPTER 28: The Stage Called Truth

"Truth in a courtroom wasn't what happened. It was what survived under fluorescent light."

By the third week of the trial, truth wasn't a destination anymore. Mumbai courtrooms were not built for truth. They were built for performance. Colonial relics where fans wheezed like they remembered Partition, and light bulbs buzzed like gossip. The kind of space where even silence echoed like a verdict left unfinished. The mic smelled faintly of sweat and disinfectant. The brass stem wobbled slightly when adjusted, like even the furniture doubted the facts.

I stood there like women have stood in living rooms explaining why they stayed, explaining why they left, explaining why they didn't cry the right way at the right time for the right audience. I had rehearsed for this. Not in mirrors, but in silence. In the way you rehearse a muscle to not flinch when touched.

Behind me, a row of journalists adjusted their phones. Court stenographers blinked like overworked typewriters. Somewhere far back, Mira sat, no notebook today, just the steady weight of observation, like a lighthouse warning ships that thought they were unsinkable.

Prosecutor Mr. Jain looked like he belonged on wedding invitations—grandfatherly, soft-voiced, deceptively kind.

"Mrs. Kapoor, thank you for your composure," he had said.

Composure was the word they used when what they wanted was a collapse. I had nodded, hands folded like I was about to light a diya at a funeral, not stand trial for emotional sedition.

"You're welcome," I said.

He started gently: "How long were you married to Mr. Kapoor?"

"Seven years," I replied.

He smiled through the arithmetic of decay: seven monsoons, seven birthdays, seven slow dissolutions.

"And would you describe the marriage as loving?"

"Publicly, yes."

There was a hush. Pens scratched that phrase like it was worth copyright.

"Privately?"

"Privately, it was survival dressed as affection."

A subtle gasp. The kind that makes a jury remember they're human.

"Did you love him?" he asked.

"I loved the idea of him."

It landed. Not with drama, but with poise. He tested another angle: "Did you hate him?"

"Never. But I resented how small I had to become to be his audience."

Not anger. Not blame. Just documentation.

Jain leaned in—not physically, but morally. "Did you ask him to stop? The jokes? The public belittlement?"

"Yes," I said. "Sometimes he did."

"And when he didn't?"

"I adapted."

That word, the most elegant indictment imaginable. *Adapted.* The gallery shifted. A few jurors looked down, suddenly unsure if their own marriages were safe.

"You're a lawyer," he reminded me.

"Yes."

"You know silence can be a weapon?"

"I know it can also be a shield."

He nodded, slowly, like a teacher who knew the student had read ahead. "You were aware of Mr. Kapoor's declining mental health, were you not?"

"I was aware of his reluctance to address it."

"You continued to support him. Appear with him. Serve him tea. You curated normalcy."

"Of course I did. What else does a wife curate when a man's decline is treated like entertainment by the very people now asking about grief?"

That one hit. No drama. Just impact.

Then, he reached the inevitable. "There was a spreadsheet, wasn't there?"

"Yes." No denial. No hesitation. No stuttering. "I catalogued emotional wounds like receipts. So, I wouldn't overspend my dignity."

A few gasps. The gallery held its breath. Someone scribbled *overspend dignity* in all caps. And then came the line he had rehearsed.

"Did your husband deserve to die?"

Time slowed. The mic buzzed. Somewhere in the back, someone's pen stopped moving. I let the silence bloom.

"No one deserves to die. Not even the ones who made you wish for their absence. And certainly not someone I once built a life around."

It wasn't an answer. It was a eulogy disguised as deflection.

He tried again. "Did you kill him, Mrs. Kapoor?"

Finally, the line. I met his eyes. Not like a suspect. Like a woman spelling a difficult word for a tired man. "No."

The judge exhaled. Jain looked at his notes as if they were betrayal dressed as stationery. One of the journalists in the back dropped a pen. And in the fifth row, Mira Rao finally blinked. Silence in a courtroom isn't emptiness. It's choreography. I smiled. Not too broadly, not falsely, just enough to signal completion, the way a dancer lifts her arms in final pose before the audience remembers to clap. In the fifth row, Mira Rao blinked.

"Did you feel relief?" he asked. "When he died?"

I answered slowly. "I felt like the performance had ended. And sometimes... that's grief too."

The gallery didn't gasp. They simply fell quiet. There was no hysteria to mock. No madness to fear. Just stillness. And it terrified them. Because they couldn't decorate me with weakness. Couldn't distort my rage into madness. Couldn't reduce my silence into guilt. I didn't unravel. I concluded.

The courtroom didn't smell like truth. It smelled like deadlines, stale air trapped between ageing ceiling fans and rotting legal files. The judge looked tired. The lawyers looked rehearsed. The public looked entertained. The prosecutor stood like a man who believed the room was already convinced. His tone was lighter, smugger, because viral perception had done half his job.

"Mrs. Kapoor," he began, "I want to return to your *behavioural consistency* after your husband's passing."

Behavioural consistency. Code for: *why didn't you shatter on command?*

I inhaled, steady. "Go ahead."

He projected one clip onto the courtroom monitor. Funeral footage of me, dry-eyed, shoulders squared. The room shifted, energy tilting toward doubt.

"Is this trauma," he asked, pausing, "or calculated dissociation?" He let the question hang, knowing it would flood the evening talk shows before I could answer.

From the back, Mira Rao's gaze bored into me—not smug, not victorious… warning. This wasn't a triumph. It was demolition.

Reva, rose, measured and merciless. Her cross dismantled the smear like a slow dismantling of brittle glass. "Under Section 101 of the Indian Evidence Act, prosecution must establish guilt beyond a doubt," she reminded. Then, pointedly: "Is selective grieving illegal?"

Jain objected, and it was overruled.

"Is lack of tears proof of crime?" she pressed.

Kripalani's forensic testimony had already conceded ambiguity. The judge scribbled notes, but his lips tightened, his disbelief recalibrating.

"The prosecution plays clips. We submit full footage." She gestured toward the court clerk. A longer video cued up: me breaking once, jaw tight, blinking away private ache at the vigil after Raghav's mother's outburst. Reva spoke without blinking: "Trauma isn't a TikTok moment. It's an atmospheric condition. It breaks differently in different rooms."

Still, I could feel it: the room wasn't entirely with me anymore. Something had shifted in the algorithm of sympathy. Outside, the crowd was turning—not into a mob, but into spectators hungry for inconsistency.

"Mrs. Kapoor, what do you inherit after Mr. Kapoor's death?"

"Debt. Litigation. His unresolved defamation cases."

Silence spread. Financial motive evaporated on record.

Reva's closing was surgical. "My client wasn't orchestrating death. She was surviving surveillance: spousal, societal, systemic." Her tone steeled. "She is not on trial for murder, Your Honour. She is on trial for composure."

She referenced Article 21 of the Constitution: the Right to Life and Personal Liberty. "Is liberty to grieve in silence not protected?" she asked.

A hush fell. This wasn't guilt anymore—it was philosophy. Jain stumbled with a rebuttal. His arguments collapsed into hollow morality. As the court adjourned, the real verdict was already public. #PoisedOrPremeditated trended on social feeds, but inside the courtroom, law clawed its ground back from prejudice.

Mira Rao walked past without acknowledgement. I knew that stare—it wasn't condemnation. It was fascination. She had tried to find guilt and uncovered conditioning. Because this wasn't a trial. It was documentation. They didn't know what to do with women like me. So they tried to define me through suspicion. But I didn't live by their definitions anymore. I edited the dictionary.

They didn't convict me. They translated me. And I spoke both fluently: *guilt* and *grammar*. They wanted collapse, I gave them choreography. They wanted confession, and I gave them closure.

I didn't cry. I constructed. Because the truth, when built properly, survives the spotlight.

***

CHAPTER 29:
The Weight of a Pause

"Verdicts were not declared. They were sculpted—slowly, in the air between two held breaths."

Truth was never spoken in Mumbai courtrooms. It was constructed as carefully as scaffolding over unfinished graves. The tribunal was an old station with a colonial façade, peeling paint, and fans that never spun fast enough. Yet today, everything inside felt deliberately cold, like a stage built to prevent grief from clouding the glass.

I hadn't worn black. Black would have been theatrical. Instead, I chose pale grey, like compromise, like middle-aged rain, like unfinished apologies. Reva sat beside me. Her presence remained still, unreadable, but I felt her thigh tense next to mine. We weren't waiting for closure. We were waiting for vocabulary. Because courts didn't hand out the truth or guilt, they handed out words. Softer than blood, easier to frame.

The jury filed in like they were borrowing shoes, with empty expressions, rehearsed by committee. People romanticise jurors; really, they were clerks with nicer chairs. The foreman unfolded the verdict paper with one razor-perfect crease. I thought of my grandmother's *saris*, folded with sharp intention. This moment was not justice. It was a performance awaiting its climax.

"In the matter of State v. Aarti Kapoor…" The judge shifted her weight, punctuation mid-sentence. "…on the charge of murder, premeditated, by means of chemical manipulation…"

"We find the defendant…" They paused so deliberately that you could feel the bowstring tightening behind the word.

"…*Not Guilty.*"

The courtroom exhaled collectively. The judge met my eyes, just once. Not pity. Curiosity. Like discovering the final chapter had a plot twist.

Her ruling was clinical: "In the absence of direct causation, absence of lethal procurement traceable to the defendant, and absence of explicit motive under the evidentiary standards established by Sections 101 and 106 of the Indian Evidence Act, the court does not find sufficient grounds to establish culpability."

Translation: They didn't know how to prosecute curated grief. They didn't have statutes for composing pain in lowercase. They didn't know how to indict a woman who'd edited her silence into syntax.

Verdict: Unproven. In this country, that was as close as a clever woman got to freedom.

They murmured procedural closure, legal disclaimers about overdose, and inconclusive evidence. No one looked satisfied. Least of all Mira. Least of all me. This hadn't been a trial. It'd been punctuation, and I cared more about syntax than endings.

Outside, dust and reporters tangled in the air. I saw Mira across the street. No press badge. No pen. Just hands folded into her saree, watching. Not angry. Not relieved. Just… unfinished.

Justice didn't arrive in verdicts. It arrived in posture: who flinched first? The courtroom emptied like a public tragedy: orderly, polite, hollow. My shoes clicked on marble as I passed beneath fluorescent justice and tired stenographers towards flashbulbs and mics masquerading as empathy.

Reporters shouted their questions. I smiled tightly, intentionally. That smile wasn't innocence. It was authorship.

Inside the courtroom, there were no cheers. But the cameras clicked "unlock." New headlines formed mid-sentence: "THE WIDOW WHO DIDN'T CRY ENOUGH," "A MURDER WITHOUT BRUISES," "VERDICT WITH SMOKE BUT NO FIRE."

None were right. None were wrong. I walked out like someone stepping out of her own obituary, still drafting the final paragraph.

*

The day after the verdict, they didn't call me innocent. They called me *marketable*. TV anchors debated my grief patterns like cricket scores. Prime-time graphics swirled with hashtags while production houses fought for rights to the narrative I hadn't even finalised.

But the real ambush came forty-eight hours later on a live talk show where I was supposed to close the loop. Aarti Kapoor, the misunderstood widow, ready for redemption in curated lighting.

Except the host wasn't alone.

At the final commercial break, they introduced an "unexpected guest." The screen split. Mira Rao's face, uncompromising, appeared next to mine, remote connection, no makeup, eyes steady.

"Aarti Kapoor, congratulations on winning the legal battle," the host smiled thinly. "But tonight… we ask… Was justice served?"

I tilted my head modestly. "Justice is a wide word... like ocean currents. It depends where you stand."

He asked if I loved my husband.

"I did."

"Was it a good marriage?"

I paused, letting it resonate. "It was educational."

"Do you kill him?"

"No," I replied, "I never thought about this."

Mira cut in before I could lace my next diplomatic smile. "You didn't kill him for survival," she said, voice unflinching. "You killed him because you hated being ecited. And the only thing that silenced his authorship… was death."

The host blinked. The production team scrambled for direction. The chat exploded online.

I answered without a tremor. "I didn't kill my husband, Mira."

"Not with poison," she said, her smile like a scalpel. "With narrative supremacy."

The moment landed. Trending in real time: #TrialByNarrative, #WhoWroteRaghavOut, #AuthorshipVsInnocence, #AartiSpeaks, #WidowOrWeapon, #GriefInHD

These weren't hashtags. They were tombstones.

*

Three nights later, a folded envelope slid under my door. Mira's handwriting, in red ink, with corrections. Inside, there was one sentence: *"I know you didn't do it for freedom. You did it for authorship."*

Tucked beside it, on a pale yellow post-it—her handwriting again, smaller this time, almost intimate:

"You're the best editor I've ever read. But one day, someone will write a draft you can't control."

For a moment, my heart stopped—not from guilt, but from the unnerving precision of it. I slid the chain lock shut, retraced my steps to the peephole, and scanned the hallway. Empty.

I read the sentence again. And again.

It wasn't a threat. It was a reminder that even authors can be outwritten.

I folded it neatly. Technique, not rage.

She wasn't chasing me anymore. She was archiving me. And that, I realised, was more dangerous than any verdict. I didn't cry. I didn't drink. I made tea in our brass kettle, the one Raghav bought impulsively in Jaipur. *"It reminds me of quiet women who make noise taste better,"* he once said.

*

They didn't forgive me. They didn't acquit me. They simply ran out of language for women like me. And that was the loophole I'd written this script for.

They cleared my name, but not my shape. Because doubt always fits better than truth.

***

PART *Five*

AUTHORSHIP & AFTERMATH

CHAPTER 30:

Blog Post—"Justice Is a Male Invention"

"Courtrooms close cases. Stories keep breathing."

I logged into my anonymous blog, where Mira probably still watched. The cursor blinked. No aliases. No softened metaphors. No mournful monologue.

I opened a new draft: *Aarti Kapoor @TheOtherHalf. Title: "Justice Is a Male Invention."*

I typed—not with tremble, but with timing. The trial was over, but the story remained mine. I hovered. Then clicked *Publish*. It felt less like rebellion, more like pulling the trigger on a meticulously planned revolution.

This wasn't a confession. It was a blueprint. A scalpel. A clarifying scream.

"The law didn't save me. I built its blueprints around myself. Men write suicide notes. Women write policy. I didn't get framed. I designed the frame, and asked them to call it guilt.

"When a man dies, they search his past. When a woman survives him, they search her motives. If she survives elegantly, without tears, without spectacle, she becomes 'complicated.' As if composure isn't something we've been forced to weaponise just to stay alive.

"Don't confuse stillness with surrender. Still waters don't run deep. They drown quietly.

"Stillness isn't innocence. It's a strategy. Don't mistake calm for forgiveness. Forgiveness is a full-time job. I already had one.

"He said I was eerie, breathed too evenly. So I showed him what happened when you held your breath long enough. You didn't just survive underwater. You dragged someone else down with you.

"I wasn't his punishment. Punishment suggests justice, a moral ledger balanced. I was something else entirely.

"I was the break in his rhythm—the moment the breath caught mid-word, the wrong note that ruins the song he thought he'd written.

"And once you've heard it, you can't unhear it.

"When men fall, we mourn them. When women rise, we audit them. I wasn't on trial for murder. I was on trial for composure. I wasn't acquitted because I was innocent. I was acquitted because I was unclassifiable.

"Justice doesn't serve women like me. We serve ourselves survival, in small curated plates: composure, silence, smile. Men leave behind estates. I left behind an architecture of grief that couldn't be bulldozed."

By the end, it wasn't a confession—it was curriculum. They demanded catharsis. I offered coursework. No hashtags. No comments. Just clarity shaped as fire. Posted at 00:01: that late-night hour when the city forgot itself. Lawyers pretended to sleep. Influencers joked in low tones. Shame was dressed in pyjamas, unaware of the alert on her phone.

I stayed awake. Not from insomnia, but from authorship. This wasn't a passive memoir or gentle footnote. It was a declaration. Justice isn't fairness—it's architecture, and architecture wasn't built for women like me.

*

By 00:07, #JusticeIsAMaleInvention hadn't trended.

By 00:11, it became a TikTok syllabus.

By 00:19, an ex-Delhi University intern had made an infographic: "Don't mistake stillness for surrender."

My inbox flooded with podcast requests, death threats, and corporate feminist retreats. A lot of noise. But then came messages from women who mattered: Doctors. Teachers. Bank tellers. Widows. Engineers. Grandmothers. *"I read your words with shaking hands," "You said what I was afraid to whisper," "You didn't just bury him. You buried how they bury us."*

I took no pride. I was operational. Publishing wasn't pride. It was plumbing. Clearing collective rot for a moment before it rose again.

The country was divided like a courtroom with no gavel: They spat: Psychopath," "Feminist terrorist," and "This is why men don't open up." They cheered: "Pattern interrupt," "Stillness ≠ submission."

*

At 02:33, the message I had awaited arrived from Mira. It said, *"You know this will burn you too."*

I read it three times. Not in fear, but in weight.

I replied with no punctuation, no drama: *"only ashes stay permanent"*

She read it. No reply. That's why I respected her. Not because she forgave me, but because she accepted me. Mira never tried to rescue me. She saved the backup of who I used to be before I rewrote the code.

Analytics refreshed. A new subscriber. Email: mira.rao@gmail.com. No picture. Just a shadow… quietly watching.

*

Then, publishing houses called. A French editor: *"Subversive feminist noir with Bhagavad Gita intensity."* I sipped wine. Laughed softly. Labelled the screenshot: "Blurbs."

At 03:16, an offer arrived: ₹85 lakh advance + film rights. I downloaded it. Renamed the PDF: *Legacy_Draft_1*. Not for money. For receipt. A proof I'd survived them all.

*

I hadn't killed Raghav to be freed. I killed because I refused to be unfinished. No courtroom could edit me better than I could edit myself.

I then wrote the final lines of the blog: "I didn't break the system. I annotated it. Footnotes always outlive the main text."

They asked for a confession. I gave them the curriculum. When the syllabus burns, chapter by chapter, someone will find Mira's redpen backup copy. That will be their closest version of the truth.

It will never be enough for them. But for me? Enough. Always enough.

***

CHAPTER 31:
How to Let Go—The Bestseller

"Some women survive by forgetting. Others survive by rewriting the story on their own terms."

It dropped at dawn. Tuesdays were preferred, the publishers had said. "Redemptive" was the word they used, like sin could be rebranded into softcover. I let them believe it was their idea.

But dawn wasn't chosen for commerce. I picked it because it was the only time Mumbai didn't pretend. Between ragpickers and residual dreams, that hour tasted like unfinished vengeance brewed in yesterday's *chai*.

The cover had come to me barefoot in the kitchen, staring at a crack that ran from the ceiling to the corner of the exhaust fan, a fracture pretending to be harmless. That's where the lotus idea began. Not from mythology. From pressure.

A white lotus blooming from concrete. They called it poetic. I called it premeditated.

The title they received was gentle. Digestible. *How to Let Go: A Widow's Guide to Emotional Survival.* Soft consonants. Pliable grief. Something you could stack next to cookbooks or healing memoirs.

The real title? I said it only in my head each time I proofread: *How to Get Away with Everything.* The subtitle was mine alone: *A Map of the Controlled Collapse.*

By 9:03 a.m., it hit #1 in Grief & Memoir. By noon, it was a pastel post on thousands of filtered Instagram feeds, a minimalist lotus hovering over serif font: *"Grief doesn't end you. It ends the illusion that others get to define your survival."*

That line? That was bait. I gave them sentences so smooth they could tattoo them without bruising. They never noticed the blades folded inside the grammar.

Reviewers called it "disarming," "measured," and "almost suspiciously poised." *Suspiciously.* That was the word that clung like steam on courtroom glass. They didn't understand. They weren't reading a memoir. They were reading a weapon disguised as a watercolour.

By the end of the first week, readers quoted me like they were citing family recipes: *"Hope is just deferred revenge in prettier packaging."*

Week two turned the book into posture. Into fashion. Into a scarf draped just so at Goa literary panels, where the women smiled too tightly and the men spoke over them gently.

But the ones who truly read it? They didn't tag me. They didn't comment. They encrypted.

One note arrived from a retired IAS officer's wife: *"You didn't just bury him. You buried how they bury us."* Another from a pharmacy student in Jaipur: *"You made silence an art. Now I know how to wield mine."*

The men fumbled. One in *The Hindu* wrote: "Aarti Kapoor has introduced a new threat: the strategic survivor. A woman who doesn't just grieve. She curates." Another tried: "Post-traumatic architecture." He meant it as praise. He didn't realise I'd underlined that phrase in red in his wife's copy.

*

I hadn't written a memoir. Memoirs heal. This was forensic. This was postmortem literature disguised in lowercase suffering. I hadn't written to inspire. I wrote to document an execution they couldn't charge me for. They asked for healing. I gave them archiving.

By week three, the most dangerous email arrived. Not from the media. Not from lawyers. From a professor in Pune. Subject: *Review Request for Academic Citation.* "We'd like to include your work in our Gender Studies syllabus. Please share citation preference."

That was the moment I knew. Real power doesn't trend. It gets footnoted.

*

Male critics couldn't classify me anymore. "She's not emotional," one wrote. "She's… designed."

Exactly. Like a courthouse. Like a legal brief. Like a crime scene that dressed itself in linen before disappearing.

Another headline read: *"She survived her husband. Then she sold the blueprint."*

They meant it with awe. They didn't realise they were part of the distribution network.

And then, as expected, came Mira, at 3:22 a.m., with no greeting, no emojis, just: *"It's not a book. It's a declaration of war."*

I stared at it the way surgeons stare at incisions they know won't scar. I typed back: *"That's what they asked for. Closure. This is what closure looks like when women write it."*

Because nobody talks about how violent closure is. It's not an ending. It's a kind of permission. And I'd written a book that let women hold a neatly folded ending in their laps like a silk *saree* never worn in public.

Mira was the only one who knew it wasn't healing. It was surgery.

*

In Bandra, over rosé and infidelities, women quoted me like they had survived something.

They hadn't. They were borrowing my tone. They thought they were part of the story. They were part of the product.

The real story was never in the highlighted quotes. It lived in the footnotes I never published. *Footnote 1: This chapter is for the girl who smiled too soon at the funeral. Footnote 2: This isn't healing. This is recalibration. Footnote 3: The only thing more dangerous than a silent woman is one who edits her grief.*

I didn't write for redemption. I wrote to file receipts. Receipts of the bruises dressed in wit. Receipts of the dignity that didn't leak. Receipts of a system that prefers women to bleed in calligraphy.

I didn't break the system. I published it. And they applauded because I gave it paragraphs and justified alignment. They never noticed the acknowledgements page, printed in faint italics, bottom right corner: *"Thank you to those who taught me restraint. I only ever weaponise what I'm taught."*

They never cared about it. Only Mira did.

*

Final line of the chapter, never printed, only spoken aloud once to myself, over chamomile tea the night before the first reading:

"They didn't give me freedom. They gave me formatting. And that was always the loophole."

***

CHAPTER 32:

The Woman Inside the Silence—The Widow's Question

"Some women sought justice. Others authored it."

Three weeks after launch, the invitation arrived cold and calculated:

Subject: Keynote: Structural Violence in Law

From: UN Women, South Asia

They said it was "an attempt to centre survivors' voices." What they meant was: *an attempt to launder their conscience through someone who didn't scream.* Reputation laundering, dressed in satin lanyards and organic fruit platters. Nothing says apology like chamomile tea served in crockery too delicate for anyone who's ever actually broken.

I accepted. Not for redemption, but for control.

The venue was in Mumbai, of course. Five-star banquet hall off Worli Sea Face. The kind of hall with white LED backlights designed to make every speech look profound, even if the speaker is choking on compromise.

Backdrop: *"Rewriting Narratives: Women Who Rise,"* soft gold font on cream. As if typography could erase trial transcripts. And there it was: My name, 12 feet high, projected across chiffon curtains like scripture written by someone who's never read violence properly.

I wore navy. Silk. Not for modesty. For armour. Hair centre-parted. No rings. Minimal eyeliner. I wanted my gaze to be sharp, not *styled*. A journalist from *Vogue* whispered:

"Minimalist elegance. Dangerous restraint." She had no idea how correct she was.

They served pomegranate spritzers. Some influencer in pastel with pearls whispered behind me, "She's iconic." They didn't understand. Iconic isn't survival. It's scaffolding.

I stepped up to the microphone like I'd been walking toward it since the trial, since the whisper campaigns, since Raghav said: *"Why don't you ever cry like normal women?"* I didn't bring grief. I brought strategy.

The first line out of my mouth wasn't a quote. It wasn't emotional. It was algebra: "Law is written by men. Survival is written by women."

Silence. Not the respectful kind. The sharp, *what-now* kind. Half the room held its breath because they were waiting for something soft. Something media-friendly. I gave them math instead.

"Justice is a word men invented to stay relevant at sentencing."

Pause. Let it land. Not in applause. In discomfort. I didn't give them hope. I gave them *procedure*. I gave them the blueprint they missed when they were printing hashtags on recycled tote bags.

"Women don't survive violence by faith. They survive it by logistics."

The woman from UN Women squirmed. Someone in the second row tried clapping early. I ignored them both.

"I didn't come here to inspire you. I came here to issue a correction. You've mistaken our ability to cry in court for weakness. What you should've been worried about was our ability to file affidavits with a trembling hand steady enough to get your laws rewritten."

The photographers started flashing like they'd caught a scandal. They'd caught *curriculum*.

A woman near the back with a silver braid and worn palms mouthed "thank you" like she was praying. Another, young, newer, still with soft wrists, barely healed, looked like she was memorising my syntax for later use in some boardroom where HR policies smell like disinfectant and dismissal letters.

I closed with this: "You don't need a gavel to finish a trial. You just need an audience that doesn't flinch when the woman doesn't apologise."

Applause. Louder than it should have been. Cheerful. Nervous. Like people congratulating a storm for arriving on time.

Afterwards, they handed me a bouquet of white lilies. I took them politely, because that's what you do when the system hands you flowers for surviving the sentence they were hoping would break you.

Someone backstage asked if I was proud. I didn't answer. Pride is a costume. I was already in uniform.

She waited near the women's restroom—not the event hall, not the glossy lobby with its imported tiles and bored security guards. No one waits for heroes by the mirrors with soap streaks. That's where real questions happen. Next to the hiss of hand dryers. Next to the places where people pretend to cry quietly.

She didn't have foundation on her face. She didn't wear defiance as posture. Just a simple *kurta* with a frayed hem, like a woman who's still folding grief into her wardrobe without meaning to.

"Hi," she said, eyes flickering toward my neckline, not to check the label, but to avoid meeting the eyes of someone who's survived what no one writes sympathy cards for. "I'm Richa. I run a free desk. Varanasi. Family courts."

No badge. No selfie request. Just a name and a city that smells of burning *ghee* and family disputes filed too late.

"I know this is awkward," she continued, "but your… case…" She paused, as if saying *case* might make me real, "—it helped me survive something that… might not have killed me, but definitely erased the parts that used to speak."

She held out an envelope. Thin. Unassuming. More dangerous than any dagger. "There's a man. Good on paper. He's been asking." Pause. "I've already started documenting him. Password-protected. Just like you taught."

I should've told her to rest. Should've said *trust is still possible.* That not every hand held in the dark carries a concealed narrative. But I didn't. I met her eyes and gave her the only truth Mumbai ever taught me:

"Never stop documenting. Even joy needs evidence."

She folded the envelope tighter like it was a lung she wasn't ready to fill yet. "I don't want to become you," she said.

I smiled. "You won't. You'll become someone *worse*."

And that was the first moment I realised: I wasn't their hero. I was their prototype.

*

Later that night, the luxury cars lined the streets outside the hall. People posed under banners about resilience. Panellists ordered vegan appetisers. Hashtags drifted upward like censored prayers.

But I was in the corner of my own apartment. Tea turning cold, knees sharp against kitchen tiles, crying. Not for Raghav. Not even for the cost of control.

I cried because I couldn't tell anymore where *I* stopped and the script began. The mirror across the room caught my reflection like it was bored with my rehearsals. This was not cinema. This was Mumbai, with its wet walls, flickering bulbs, and grief treated like background noise at traffic signals.

And then came clarity, not comfort. Because after everything, I couldn't tell if I had ever wanted justice… or just the power to choose when I would stop pretending. The apartment was silent, but inside my chest, there was an unfamiliar emptiness, like a house stripped bare after the guests leave, echoing with forgotten voices.

I crawled to the mirror. Saw a woman with hollowed cheekbones and eyes that had memorised too much grief to ever return to softness. I whispered—half to myself, half to the woman staring back: "You didn't kill him for freedom. You wrote yourself out of a sentence you never deserved."

The spreadsheet had started as a strategy. It ended as a curriculum. Women didn't need confessions anymore. They needed solutions.

*

That night, I couldn't sleep. Not from guilt. From awakening. You don't feel remorse when your tool finally works. You feel alignment.

The file hadn't even gone viral. That wasn't the point. This wasn't virality. It was velocity. They wanted a survivor. I gave them a syllabus. They wanted a widow. I gave them a bestseller. But what they still don't understand is that murder isn't an end. It's a method. And silence… is the only genre worth rewriting. Women weren't quoting me anymore. They were upgrading me. And somewhere, another story was being written. Not about justice, but about how silence became the most dangerous weapon of all. Not to find relief, but to begin her own version of the ending.

***

Epilogue

They thought it was over. That I'd said everything I had to say. That after the trial, the book, the keynote, I would vanish back into stillness.

But stillness was never silence. It was set up. They never heard my voice. Not really. When I spoke, it was too soft. When I stayed silent, it was too cold. So I stopped offering them temperature.

One night, at 2:17 a.m., while the city slept under the illusion of men like him, I uploaded a PDF from a burner email and a trembling hand. There was no picture. No ISBN. No dedication. Just stories: essays, court transcripts, fragments of jokes, emails, poetry, spreadsheets, and silence. Silence dissected like pathology. I called it *The Perfect Widow.*

I didn't attach my name. I wanted the words to walk on their own, unburdened by a woman's face, judged only by their precision.

Within hours, it spread like gossip, but landed like gospel. They tried to guess who wrote it. Some said it was fiction. Some said it was vengeance. They weren't wrong.

It took the internet exactly five hours to realise who had written it. At first, they denied it. Then, they devoured it. Threads appeared. Think-pieces multiplied. Raghav Kapoor's jokes were re-watched, now with discomfort. The laughter didn't land the same anymore.

A viral reel slowed one of his routines down frame by frame: the line where he mocked my panic attacks. The likes turned into questions. The applause became posthumous guilt.

Followers became historians. He became what he feared most: a man whose punchline outlived its welcome. They called it a reckoning. I called it… recalibration.

Book clubs began to read *The Perfect Widow* aloud as testimony, not literature. Men called it a witch hunt. Women called it scripture.

The publisher, whom I never contacted, printed it under "Recovered Works." It sold 3 million copies in 4 months. All proceeds went to a foundation she never took credit for. But I didn't stay to collect applause. I had no interest in becoming a symbol. I'd had enough of being framed.

So, I left the noise behind.

And now? Now I live off-grid. No camera lenses, no courtrooms, no captions. I don't wear lipstick anymore. I sit across from the women you will never hear about. I teach them how to speak without saying sorry. I teach them where to hide files, where no man ever thinks to look. I wear stillness like armour now. I don't raise my voice. I raise others.

And still... You want an ending.

You think there's a final page that can tell you whether I was right. Whether Raghav's death was right? Whether Dev ever left that holding cell... Or whether someone made sure he wouldn't walk out again. You want to know if justice was served, or sabotaged. You asked for a confession. You wanted closure.

But I told you from the beginning: this isn't a crime story. It's a curriculum.

And if you've reached this far, if you're still reading between the headlines, still searching for closure, then maybe you're not just a reader anymore. Maybe you're the next file.

And if you've made it this far... You're probably already editing your version of the file. But that's the real ending. Not a body in a bathtub. Not a smile in a press photo. Not a trial or a trending thread.

The real ending is this: he turned me into content. I turned myself into code. And now I run quietly in the background of every woman you think you can't erase.

***

Acknowledgements

Writing *The Perfect Widow* was as much an act of reflection as it was of storytelling. I don't owe this book to inspiration—I owe it to the women whose stories of resilience, survival, and clarity reminded me that truth doesn't always scream—it often waits patiently for its moment. To the readers who underline the uncomfortable lines instead of skipping them, thank you for proving that crime isn't about bodies, it's about power. To friends who endured endless conversations about "what makes a perfect crime" and offered their laughter when I needed relief. And most importantly, to the *Nu Voice Press* team, whose faith, meticulous effort, and creative vision transformed a manuscript into a book that could truly find its audience. Your belief in this story means everything.

***

About the Author

Deepak Trivedi is a veterinary science graduate based in Punjab, where he works as a manager with a multinational corporation while actively supporting dairy farmers through his professional expertise. Alongside his career, he has established himself as a prolific writer with a deep interest in crime fiction and motivational literature.

With a passion for crime fiction, Deepak has emerged as a distinctive voice in the genre, exploring the darker layers of relationships, silence, and survival. His debut novel, *How to Kill Your Wife*, was noted for its gripping psychological depth and sharp narrative. His latest, *The Perfect Widow*, continues this journey—an unsettling tale of power, satire, and calculated revenge.

In his personal time, Deepak enjoys reading classic and contemporary crime novels, painting, and experimenting with new recipes in the kitchen. His diverse interests and professional experiences bring a unique perspective to his writing, making his novels both engaging and thought-provoking.

***